Metaphorosis

August 2020

Beautifully made speculative fiction

Also from Metaphorosis

Verdage

Reading 5X5 x2: Duets
Score – an SFF symphony
Reading 5X5: Readers' Edition
Reading 5X5: Writers' Edition

Metaphorosis Magazine

Metaphorosis: Best of 20xx
Metaphorosis 20xx: The Complete Stories
annual issues, from 2016

Monthly issues

Plant Based Press

Best Vegan Science Fiction & Fantasy
annual issues, from 2016

from B. Morris Allen:
Susurrus
Allenthology: Volume I
Tocsin: and other stories
Start with Stones: collected stories
Metaphorosis: a collection of stories

Metaphorosis

August 2020

edited by
B. Morris Allen

ISSN: 2573-136X (online)
ISBN: 978-1-64076-175-9 (e-book)
ISBN: 978-1-64076-176-6 (paperback)

Metaphorosis
a magazine of speculative fiction
from
Metaphorosis Publishing

Neskowin

August 2020

Calling Me Home

Spencer Nitkey

The entanglement circuit burns as it lights a fire right behind my eyes. I hear my daughter crying in the moments before the circuit switches. An imagined voice, I'm sure. Then the pain spreads like blood through my chest, and the stars outside the transport ship window slow, stop, and disappear.

I come to in my bed back home. The baby monitor plays a low whine that crescendos into a full-scale cry. It is the first thing I hear back in this body. I put my hand on my husband's back as he grunts and starts to sit up.

"It's okay. I've got it," I tell him, tripping over my old tongue.

I get up and stumble, still not sure footed in my old body. I lean against the hallway wall to catch my balance. In Altair's room, I sit in the rocking chair near the crib, and hold Altair in the crook of my arm and feed her. I hope this is what she wants. I love Altair so deeply. She is beautiful and strange, but her wants are foreign to me. I am, I guess, stabbing in the dark. She focuses, her whole face pressed together in concentration, on sucking the formula from the bottle. I breathe a sigh of relief. She was hungry. I helped fix it. This is worth every bit of the discomfort it takes to transfer, even if just for a few hours. It's rare they let me take an unscheduled transfer home.

"It's okay," I whisper. The sun is rising, and the sounds of early commuters slowly roar until the noise-cancellation flicks on and there's an ambient quiet again. I sit Altair in a high chair near the kitchen table and pour boiling water over the coffee grinds in the French press.

My husband comes out when the chestnut crepes are almost done cooking. He looks exhausted. I'm sure I do too, the weariness carried over from my spaceskin to this one. It is nice to be working with small and delicate things for a moment. The small flick of the knife, the gentle rocking of Altair, all so different from the lumbering weight of the minerals, mining equipment, and explosives I work with in the Belt. I enjoy this smaller, more sensitive body in these small spurts.

"Is it Saturday, already?" he asks.

"No. I get a few hours break during the trip from Ceres to Hygiea and thought I'd surprise you," I answer.

"I'm glad you did," he says as he kisses my forehead. "It's nice to see you for a little while, at least." The words sound like drill bits snapping, and I take it too personally.

"Well, we need money don't we?" I say. He tightens his jaw, and I watch it loosen. He slouches, then takes a few steps back from me, like he is about to apologize for my shortness. Communicating back home is always hard. The bodily adjustments are one thing, but moving seamlessly from a military-style mining operation to domestic conversation is hard. In the Belt, there are clear goals, and in my skin I can achieve each and every one of them. It's an intoxicating feeling. Here on earth, my body adjusts quickly. My mind doesn't.

I turn to Altair, who is making slurping noises, harvesting drool from her hands back into her mouth. She still makes no sense to me—a confluence of atoms and biology and accident that resulted in this: the most beautiful thing I've ever seen— but still, I love her. I am on my toes around her, waiting for the leg of her chair to tip, a piece of food to lodge in her fragile throat, but she is mine, and so are the doubt and uncertainty she casts on me.

My husband takes a large bite of crepe and doesn't say anything. I regret our tiff already, he's so handsome in the morning light, but the circuit behind my head beeps, and I have five minutes to lie back down in bed and get ready for the return.

He winces when the sound rings through the kitchen. The baby starts crying and he takes her in his arms and kisses me on the forehead. The circuit jolts to life and I feel the heat of it already.

"I love you," I say.

"I love you, too."

I crawl into bed, lay down, close my eyes, and wait.

I'm so tired I think my mechanized space-skin is about to crack open and let the small ooze of me leak out like a spilled drink. My biological brain is resting, sleeping, emptied and recovering, in my body back home, and this skin doesn't need sleep to flush protein buildup the same way biological brains do. My physical body sleeps all the time, it's just my consciousness that doesn't. I am awake nearly 24 hours a day, especially when working. Still, I am tired; I want static nothingness just for a few hours. I don't have time, though. I have been hearing Altair cry all day, her small voice ricocheting through the wiring and the acoustic chamber that replicates my ears. I know I can't actually hear her, but this memory of her voice feels like it is calling me back to Earth. Even with all the hell I am going through on Hygiea, her voice is all I think about, more than the alignment on the sonic drill, or tension in the tether, or the carrying capacity of the supply train.

I clock out for my hour off, and already the entanglement circuit is spinning. I try to swallow the spreading pain and imagine the trillion spinning photon-like particles that make up my mind in the circuit that are moving a trillion other, entangled particles in my brain back home, lying in bed. The sun blooms inside me, and the inside of the transport ship vanishes.

I wake up to the sun setting through the open window. Warm summer air washes over my skin. I roll over and look at the clock. It's 8:00 pm. I hear the faint sounds of television, and walk out into the living room, unsteady, eyes drooping low.

"You're up!" my husband whisper-shouts, careful not to scare Altair, when he hears me creaking towards him. He wraps me up, tightly, and I feel like all my fraying parts are being pulled back together.

"I was worried I'd miss you," he says. "How are you doing? Can I get you something?"

"A drink, please," I say.

"I have an open bottle of red?"

"Stronger."

He pours me a few fingers of my good whiskey, which he never drinks. He looks concerned as I down it in one sip.

"Everything alright?"

I can't hold any of it back. "Hygiea is a nightmare. Chock full of palladium, so our targets are sky-high, but so small the gravity's just nothing. Even in the suit, we have to do everything tethered, so it's all twice as hard and four times as slow. We were supposed to get a week off—"

"Claire no —" he interrupts. He already knows where this is going, and I can see the joy fall from his face.

"But it's looking like we're not even getting a weekend, and our week is being deferred until we hit our targets," I finish the thought. I hate disappointing him. I hate not being able to tell him how I feel about him. How thoughts of him keep my wiring warm in the freeze of the belt. How thoughts of his voice comfort me almost as much as thoughts of Altair. How I think about the first meal he cooked me when I am mining and want nothing more than to taste something even though I'm never hungry. How I thank him quietly every time I transfer for quitting his career as a software engineer to raise Altair while I work.

"I'm sorry," he says, and I can't help but wonder what he's sorry for. For me? For himself? For Altair? Now that our reunion is dampened, I can see how tired he looks beneath the effort he puts on to hide it. The bags under his gray eyes make them look like waning moons with long shadows. His wrinkles seem deeper set. He hasn't been sleeping. He's skinnier, his arms slightly deflated, and he has a small pouch, or the beginnings of one. I wish I had the energy to tell him how gorgeous he looks. He is going to age well, I think.

"It's just hard to be a single parent all the time," he says, rinsing his wine glass in the kitchen. "Do you ever regret it?"

I still have four more years of this on my contract that I signed when I was eighteen. I remember the recruiter in a crisp suit calling me over to his booth at the high school college fair. When he told me the company could pay for all four years of my undergraduate degree and then give me five years of work experience, guaranteed, I thought he was making fun of me. When he didn't laugh, I almost cried with joy, I was so happy to sign. I remember the hours I spent in the entanglement surgery 12 months before my ship-out date. I was already pregnant, but they said it would be fine. They installed the circuit. They opened my skull and targeted the sixteen trillion particles they found that contained my consciousness. They passed a laser through them and entangled them with the neural-processing center of my space skin and then installed the circuit that could agitate them simultaneously, creating a line of communication and transfer. They shipped my space skin to Ceres and I had one year to enjoy earth before my skin arrived and I would transfer.

Franklin doesn't understand why I'm not more upset. And I am upset, but not like he is. I don't know how to explain it. Home, I feel weak and tired. I don't know what I'm doing here. I love Altair, but I don't know how to love her right. I don't know what I'm doing when I hold her, but I hold her as often as I can, like it's all I've ever known how to do. Then, when I transfer, suddenly, I'm unstoppable. There are clear, concrete objectives. Build this. Carry that. Extract this much. And I can do it. Everything they ask of me, I can do. My body moves intentionally. It is intoxicating: waking up from uncertainty into the skin of a superhero and knowing exactly what my job is.

And would I take a different deal? I don't think so. If I'd known every gory detail the recruiter neglected to tell me, 18-year-old me would have ran the other way. The me now couldn't leave everything

I've gained behind. I met Franklin at a college in Philadelphia I could have never afforded on my own. I remember his dumb smile beaming across the library from behind a tattered copy of Chekhov stories, and I am glad I made the deal, despite everything. I look over at Altair, sitting on a high chair, and I am glad that I had the chance to make something so perfect with Franklin. Despite all the pain, it's hard to look at them and consider ever giving it up.

"If there were a way out, would you even take it?" he asks, tired of waiting for me to respond.

"I only have an hour," I say, in lieu of addressing his point. It's not worth thinking about an impossibility. "Can I change her? She smells." I should apologize, but there's nothing I can do about it. I signed a contract. He married me. Here we are. I try to remember that and hope he can, too.

"Of course you can," he says. "That'd be really nice." It's an act of love. He lets me feel like a parent when I have no right to.

I set Altair on the changing table, and her feet are small. My husband watches over my shoulder as I coo. She is a beautiful, profoundly magical person. The fact that I made her seems—especially as I am now, barely functional in my own skin —impossible.

When I'm done, I spend an hour holding Altair close to me, as close as I can. I stare for a very long time at her face as a movie plays softly. I try to interpret the thoughts and emotions that pass through her. Her brow furrows and I wonder if she is trying to decipher the look on my face, like I am trying to decipher the look on hers. The hour passes quickly this way. Then the circuit chimes on the back of my head. I hand her back to my husband and head towards the bedroom. He kisses my forehead, like he does every time we say goodbye. Even when we are fighting.

The circuit fires and my bedroom disappears. The last sound I hear is Altair babbling to my husband. "Goodbye," I whisper.

Moses died on the rig today, so witnesses get an afternoon of mourning time to spend with our families. They don't say this, but I know we also get time off because we already reached our weekly goals. If we were behind, it wouldn't matter how many people died: we'd still be working. I'm numb from it, so I hardly notice the transfer.

When I come to, I am in the bedroom with the blinds drawn, my feet still in stirrups from the negatrophic workout my bed just finished. I fish my feet out of the metal loops, and lie there for a few minutes. I don't have the energy or inclination to get up. I didn't realize how much I loved the psychic comfort of sleep until now. Now that it's denied to me.

I was there when it happened, when Moses died. The images of it reoccur to me, now. His tether broke loose and wrapped around his sternum. We had warned the company about faulty tethers, but they hadn't listened. When the anchor pulled down, it practically sliced him in half. I watch the last minutes of it in my memory—I watch his electric eyes flicker, lose power, and fade forever. As I watched Moses die, Altair's cries sang in the background and I couldn't understand anything about my life for a few minutes. If I'd had lungs, I'm sure I would have been hyperventilating.

They warned us when we first shipped out: if we aren't transferred out of a skin and it gets destroyed, our consciousness putters out, too. Someone is supposed to be monitoring us as we work, to avoid things like this, but Moses's death confirms what we all suspect: the company is either too short-staffed or too indifferent to really monitor us. Be careful, they told us. Be smart. And we do feel invincible in the suits. The first day, I remember the rush. So strong and sturdy. We walked as steel monsters and were proud. When he died, I watched Moses's biomatter, a dense tangle of neural cells congealed near his circuit, where they inserted the trillions of entangled consciousness particles, float into the vacuum of space. Rescue reached him after the tether broke and tried to initiate a transfer, but by then there was nothing left *to* transfer. I imagine his body back home, a vacant, mindless husk someone still has to kill and bury. Company men will knock on the door, and his wife will answer it and not really understand. She won't know he died until the company tells her. His heart will still be beating, his lungs pumping air in and out of his blood. He will die twice. The company won't tell his wife that he died because they wouldn't replace the tethers, even though we have been begging for new ones for months. They will just tell her he's dead, and let her do the dirty work.

You'd think that watching someone die in a mech-suit wouldn't be traumatic. There's no blood, no guts—just screws, tubes and steaming pistons, the small grey film of their mind wavering like petals to the dirt. But when that person was your friend, when you've known him for five years and, to you, he's only ever been that suit, it really isn't any better than watching a human body get torn apart: it's still death.

The house is quiet. I notice that the baby monitor isn't on and when I look for it on the bedside table it isn't there either. I get up to explore. No one is home, I realize pretty quickly. My chest buzzes with sadness.

I look for a note and find one stuck to the fridge with a magnet.

"Visiting my parents, call if home. Love, Franklin."

I miss my husband, of course, but I hurt for Altair. Her absence shocks like a faulty battery, sharp, alive, electric. I open all the blinds in the house to let the night in. The sky is like an over-washed blanket; the stars, a hundred odd holes torn through the fabric. I look up and try to find my other body, vacant in a transport pod somewhere in the asteroid belt. I try to swallow the sadness, keep it from staying lodged in my throat.

I lie on my back on the asphalt of the driveway outside. Is it even worth calling him? I'll be gone again before I could make the trip to his parents. What good would it do either of us? A rushed conversation? A glimpse of each other's faces? Apologies that wouldn't change anything? I want to see him, but I don't want to fight about something I can't change. I don't want to be reminded of all the pain I cause someone I love.

I need to see Altair though, so I call. The line rings and rings. I'm ready to give up when Franklin answers, and his face fills the camera, shadowed with stubble and wild eyebrows.

"Claire!" he shouts, a little drunk. "You're home. How long?"

"Half-day," I mutter.

"Oh. So you can't make it?"

"No, I'm sorry," I say.

"They let you off for my birthday?" he asks. "I'm sorry, if I had known, we wouldn't have left."

Shit. I hadn't even realized. Time takes on such an ethereal, useless quality in space. It's not grounded in anything, so it's easy to lose track of.

"No," I say. "Just a lucky coincidence," half-heartedly, in a way I am sure betrays the truth.

"Do you want to see Altair?" he asks. If he knows that I forgot, he doesn't say anything. I want to thank him for this, but don't know how. There's so much I don't know how to do.

Altair suddenly fills the blurry screen, a hundred or so pixels of her. Still, there she is. Wisps of brown hair dot her smooth head. Her eyes blink confusedly and look nowhere in particular. I can see her chubby fingers smack at the phone. God, she's smart, I think. And for a minute or two I don't think about, or see, anything other than her, this little person who is already so much better than I am. The blinker on my neck flashes and I tell my husband I have to go.

"Happy birthday, baby," I say as he takes the phone back. "I love you."

Later, I hold the phone on my chest as the circuit flashes. I try to think of her, and hope maybe I will hear her voice in the Belt again.

It is Altair's first birthday today, exactly fourteen days after Franklin's, and I do get this day off. I am a little late. There were loose charges near the sonic drill, more faulty equipment the company had been too cheap to replace. Their anchors had to be repaired, and I was the only one active in the sector, so I ended up working three more hours before I clocked out. Three more hours away from Altair and Franklin. The whir of the entanglement circuit cuts me across space and I wake up to the sound of muffled laughter, footsteps, and the smell of roasted garlic.

I swivel out of bed but stay in the room for a moment. The afternoon air is stale, and the light from the sun filters through dust particles, a thin curtain of sparkling light. My husband's computer is closed next to the domestic transfer station that activates my circuit when they call me back to the Belt. Downstairs thrums with houseguests. I peek my head out from the stairwell and I watch Altair recognize me, slung over her father's shoulder. She garbles something incoherent and magical. My chest erupts like an ignited engine. Franklin's sister is the first to see me. Soon everyone is crowded around me except Franklin.

Altair is passed from one parent to another until she ends up in my arm. I field questions and side-hugs from friends and neighbors and family. I try to remember how to talk to people who aren't coworkers. I ask them questions about their children, and try to keep them talking so I don't have to; most oblige.

I realize how little I know about them. I didn't realize I was socially isolated from Earth until now. Nine months into the program, and I'm already a stranger to everyone I was friends with before. In the Belt, everything is more urgent. Each day is a navigation around death. The minerals we extract fuel everything on earth. And I'm supposed to care about barbecues, preschool teachers, and Home Owners' Association rules. I try, today. I really do.

I find Franklin, finally, and slide up next to him, pressing Altair between us. When I am feeling far from him, or when we are fighting, reminding each other of Altair helps. It's nice to remember the things that our love, done right, can make. He smiles and plays with Altair's feet.

"Have you checked for any packages recently?" I ask him.

"No. I've been a little busy setting everything up," he says. "Where were you?"

"Work," I answer. "Where else?"

"You were supposed to be here," he says, which is true.

"What did you want me to do about it?" I ask. "They weren't going to sign off until I finished loading—" I stop myself. "You don't care," I snipe. Which is both fair and unfair.

I take Altair and walk to the front door to check the porch for packages. A box with my company's logo printed on it is sitting there. I squat low to the ground and, with my free arm, pick the box up and bring it into the kitchen. I watch Franklin's face turn ghost-white at the sight of the logo. Fear, more than anything else. But I am too excited to care. I ask his sister for the pair of scissors we keep in the pantry and cut the box open.

I am giddy for the first time all day since watching Altair recognize me. With everyone watching me, I pull out a shimmering silver-colored locket, and I beam. There's another, smaller box that I take and slide into my pocket.

"It's a palladium, iridium, and ruthenium alloy," I announce to everyone, but really only to Franklin. "It's from my first haul in the Belt. I got to set aside a little metal from the first mining operation I was a part of. This is from space, Altair. It's why I've been so far from you. It's yours now."

I look up from Altair hoping to see Franklin smiling. He is. But there are no wrinkles on the corners of his eyes. It is even and not lopsided slightly to the right. His eyebrows are flat. It looks nothing like his real smile and I feel things break in me, like a thousand whirring gears and pistons all snapping in the wrong direction. I hold my breath for four seconds, trying to steady it, and look down at Altair. Her chubby fingers swipe at the chain, and her eyes reflect the shine of it. I watch the small dance of curiosity as she writhes. I let the joy of her set my gears back in place. I don't really look at anyone but her for the rest of the party.

After the last guest leaves, we clean the house in quiet. Normally, I'd ask him to play some music on the speaker, something to cut against the tension that stretches between us; the air itself taut and pulled back in to a thin, breakable surface. Now, we clean in silence. I am afraid to ask. Speaking the right words seems impossible right now.

We put Altair to bed early. She is exhausted from the party. So are we. Beneath the cool blue light of the television, my husband and I sit up in our bed.

"You know," I say. "There was one more thing in the box that got delivered today."

"Oh?" he says, half-listening.

I reach into my bedside table, beneath the entanglement port and pull out the small box and open it.

I take the small ring and turn it over in my hand. Two thin strips of platinum vine around each other until they reach the head where they prong out and enwrap a moissanite diamond. I put it in his hand, and already it is refracting the bedside table lamp in a dozen directions. He looks up at me.

"It was supposed to get here in time for your birthday," I say. "The platinum is from Ceres. And the stone is from a meteorite crater on Vesta." He looks up at me. "I know this is hard. And I'm sorry I'm not here. And I'm sorry I'm not a better wife or mom. It's a small comfort, but I think about you all the time, Franklin."

"I think about you, too," he says, rolling the ring around his hand. He gets up and turns the ceiling light on and looks at the brilliant stone beneath the light. I see tears in his eyes. "It's really beautiful, Claire."

"Think about me mining when you look at it," I say.

We kiss. I get to sleep. I get to sink beneath the sheets and let the cotton warm my skin. The dark comes over me and the first few times I'm about to lose consciousness, I flinch, expecting the shuddering jolt of transfer, but each time it doesn't come, I relax a little more. A little around midnight, I fall asleep. I am certain I was smiling.

Around 4am the baby monitor begins speaking in a loud voice. *Altair's temperature has exceeded 102 degrees. Current at-home-remedies are having minimal effect. Immediate transfer to medical professional recommended. Immediate transfer to medical professional recommended.* We both run out of bed and into Altair's room. Franklin checks her temperature manually. While he is gone for the thermometer, I put my hand against her head and pretended I know what temperature her head normally feels like. When the thermometer returns 102.2 degrees, we hurry into the car and set the autopilot to the closest emergency room.

I turn off the autopilot in the car, so we can rush to the hospital. Franklin holds Altair. He rocks and coos to her as I speed through the empty lanes of traffic. The street lights fill the road with cones of yellow light, and I cycle through every catastrophe I can imagine. Franklin is immersed in the moment, taken up entirely by Altair. Her crying hits my periphery for a moment and I tear up. I wipe my eyes and focus on the road.

When we finally get to the emergency room, I drop Franklin and Altair by the door and then find parking. As I back in to the first open spot I find, I hear the circuit's beep. I flinch. Then, I feel the vibration at the back of my skull. The circuit call shudders my bones. My heart races uncontrollably. The company wasn't supposed to call me back for another three days. I am miles from home and my baby is dying.

I am far from home, so the authentication signal from the domestic transfer station will take slightly longer to reach my circuit. Maybe I have six minutes instead of five. I run into the hospital and Franklin and Altair have already been taken to an exam room. I try to ask where they are, but I can hardly talk through the beeping in my head. It rings and rings. I feel like I'm losing control of my body. My heart is beating too fast. My breaths are shallow, lungs catching on my ribs with each hitched exhalation. I am sweating too. My body is incoherent. So are my words. Altair could be dying, and I am going to be thrown from this body in minutes. Maybe seconds now. I can hear the entanglement circuit whir to life; the authentication signal reached the circuit. I am crying inconsolably on the ground, screaming Altair's name. I try to hold on, weld my consciousness to this brain. I scream as the edges blur. There's no holding on. The last thing I think I hear is Altair's crying, then I'm gone.

As soon as I'm conscious in my spaceskin I try to talk to my supervisor. I need to be sent back, I tell her, my child is sick. She tells me that my child will be sick whether or not I am there, and the company needs me in the Belt. A rush order for a Lunar base came in and without Moses, there was no way they could fill it in time. Everyone needs to make sacrifices. I can spare an eighteen-hour shift of mining to help my team-members out, she tells me. I get to work.

All I can think about is Altair, which makes the work slower, which makes me think more about Altair. I'm used to getting lost in my labor, worries and anxieties melting in the mechanized concentration. Today, Altair's small, failing body hovers, already a phantasm, near everything.

Twenty-hours later, after we've loaded the processing ship with a full order of palladium, I get approved for a transfer. My supervisor enters her approval key, and the circuit embedded in my spaceskin's neck whirs to life. It takes longer than normal to transfer out this time. I wonder if that's because my body is still far from the transfer station. I wait for the signal to reach my body.

Then it happens all in one, whirring hot instant, and I come to in a hospital with a face already wet with tears. My rediscovered lungs are already spasming. I turn hard, and almost fall out of the bed.

Franklin puts his hand on my shoulder and I look up. The sun rising through the window behind him means I only see him in silhouette. When he leans closer to me, I see the sleeplessness tattooed across his face. I wonder if, in a few years, when I'm home, those lines and bags will fade. I hope they don't. I don't ever want to forget what he did for us, for Altair. These tired imperfections are, almost, brushstrokes. I want to kiss him. The tears come harder.

"Altair?" I manage to ask.

Franklin twists and lifts Altair out of a crib nearby. He brings her down towards me.

"She's fine. Doctors think it was a stomach bug or something. She's okay now. Her temperature fell really quickly. She's okay."

I am crying over Altair and holding her as close to my chest as I possibly can.

"I can't do this anymore," I say. "I just can't. It's too much. It's too much. I'm sorry. I can't."

My husband takes me and Altair home. I am still crying sporadically. When I can talk, I say I'm done. I say I can't imagine going back. My husband lets autopilot drive us slowly home while he holds me and runs his fingers through my hair.

"It'll be okay," he says.

"How the fuck is this going to be okay?" I whisper, and then I start crying again.

He pauses for a moment. I watch him think, calculate variables, check two sides of an equation to see if they are equal.

"I have a, well, it's not a solution, but it might be part of one," he says.

"What are you talking about, Franklin?" I say, exhausted.

"Let me show you when we get home."

Our car pulls in the driveway and Franklin helps me inside. I am still carrying Altair. My ankle hurts. When I transferred out, a nurse caught my head from hitting the floor, but my ankle twisted under the weight of my body as it collapsed. As we walk inside our home, I refuse, silently, to put Altair down. The pain in my ankle oscillates with the extra weight, but that doesn't matter. It's my job to keep Altair safe. I keep the warmth of her pressed up against me, desperate, as Franklin leads me into the bedroom.

He opens his computer, still on the bedside table next to the transfer port. He opens a screen with lines and lines of code flashing across it.

"What is this?" I ask.

He pauses for a minute. I recognize this face. He is deciding how best to explain something simply without dumbing it down too much to offend me. It's one of my favorite things he does, though I haven't seen it since I shipped out. There hasn't been much time for casual conversation; almost everything we talk about now revolves around Altair or my work.

"Well, look, you can only ever transfer with supervisor approval, right?"

"Right?"

"Well, that means there's some kind of authentication that needs to happen—"

I think I know where this is going, and I also know it's a dead end, and highly illegal. "I know, but there's no way to—" I say before he interrupts me.

"Let me finish," he says. He's excited. There's a manic energy in his eyes. "So they authenticate to transfer you home, from the Belt, but then how do they send you back without an authentication here, on Earth? Well, I wondered that for a while. I wondered if maybe when they called you back, they entered a second authentication, which wouldn't help us at all. But I started to think more. And tinker with that port there. They don't authenticate twice, because then they'd have to transfer the code back to Earth and then into this port, which is a redundancy they'd try to avoid. So I checked. It turns out what they're doing, and this is actually pretty cool, is essentially sending a second authentication with you when you transfer. It's—" he pauses for a moment to watch if I'm following. I've stopped crying, engrossed in what he's been saying. "—essentially a return ticket. They embed it with the consciousness data transfer but store it here, in the transfer station. So when they call you back, they just have to agitate the entangled particles in your spaceskin, and your consciousness particles here will automatically start their transfer spin. Which means—" By now he's gesticulating wildly, like he did when he came home with a new program solution, before he stopped working to take care of Altair. "—that if we copy that return ticket, and embed it in your consciousness data, we can send you back with an extra authentication. You could transfer on your own!" He finishes with a flourish of his hands.

"But of course it's encrypted, right?" I ask, still in disbelief that he's thought this much about it.

"It's a simple encryption. I don't think they thought anyone would bother to try to copy an authentication key, anyway. Why would they? Besides, they hire engineers and athletes, not coders. It'd be easy to fake a new one."

I don't respond for a minute. I don't say anything. It's ridiculous, hardly worth trying. Besides, even if I did it once, the company would know and be furious. The house beeps to let us know the car is done charging. The noise brings tears to my eyes. I paw, for a moment, at my skull, thinking I was being called back already. My heart rate shoots up.

"You say you can't do this anymore. This is a way out," Franklin says.

"No," I say, looking down at Altair, nestled in the crook of my arm. Her face beams up at me. I remember giving birth to her six months before shipping out. The realization washed over me as I heard her cry in the doctor's arms. I had made a person. Her skin was purple and dense. Her whole head was squeezed and elongated, like a bottle of soda. I loved her in a way that rearranged me. I loved her in a way that was older than her two hours, a love that stretched back to my first thoughts. I had built her, particle by particle. We bled into each other for nine months, mixed indelibly, a different kind of entangled and here she was for the first time on her own. She was mine and she wasn't. I was hers and I wasn't. I had made her. She had remade me. Not everyone loves their child right away, but I did. Between the bleating heart monitors, beneath the blinding fluorescence, she was perfect. She cried. That was the first noise she made, and it, too, was perfect, entangled forever in my heart.

I look down at her and see all that, for a moment, all the molecules we shared, and how far I have to be from her. I looked up at Franklin, my husband, the man who has been raising her every minute while I was away. I thought of the countless small crises he's dealt with, without me there to hold him, without me working late into the night trying to find him a way out.

I kiss Franklin. "I love you," I say. "This is insane. But you're right. It's the beginning of the way out."

I use my metal fingers to disconnect the tether from my hip. I weave the charge I stole from the shipment vessel inside the vacancies in my chest. Without a tether on, I squat low and push off, hard. Hygiea is small, its escape velocity microscopic. I fly free out of its delicate orbit, and drift. The goal is to get as far as possible from Hygiea before I blow the charge. The Belt is dense, and if I can disappear into a thousand small pieces, they'll think I was dashed to pieces against a thousand small asteroids. I don't want to transfer out of my skin whole and risk them finding it and salvaging the neural matter. I want a permanent solution.

I spin out of control, and the vertigo is unavoidable. I experience sensations I didn't know these spaceskins were capable of feeling: nausea, palpitations, arthritic pain in the freezing joints. I can barely open my fingers without silent shouts of pain. I don't eat in the skin, but I feel like throwing up, dry-heaving from the lack of stable vision. I reach out to try and grab something, anything, but my hands move through air. I struggle to remember what to do next.

I think of Altair and everything slows, crystallizes. I start the countdown on the charge, then reach towards the neck of my space skin and fish out the circuit, careful not to disconnect its wiring from the suit. I hold it as delicately as I can between my three thick metal fingers. I have to trust that Franklin's code gave me a return authentication. That my envelope engineering will work, and I am far enough from Hygiea by now that they won't know I blew myself up. I have to trust him. I'm lucky that I do. As the charge blinks silently out from my chest, I pull my left eye out of its socket, exposing the live wires beneath. Even with an authentication key, without the spark that comes with a supervisors transfer approval, the circuit needs electricity to start. I take the wire to the small battery of the circuit and hope this works. It whirs to life. My space skin swims wildly through space as my vision fades one final time. The stars and asteroid belt disappear. I taste the sensation of my limbs, the strength and fortitude of my body one last time and then, just like that, I am gone. Flown back to my body on earth, opening my eyes in my bedroom, Franklin and Altair waiting for me.

When the company comes, they come with lawyers instead of police. They beg me not to sue them for the faulty tether and almost killing me, and I graciously oblige. A real investigation might reveal what we did. Instead they "forgive" the rest of my contract. It would maybe take longer than the remaining four years on my contract to develop, entangle, and ship a new spaceskin to the belt anyway. They pay me the remainder of the contract and we go our separate ways. OSHA makes the third deep-space visit in its history, and the company is forced to dramatically increase its safety standards. Maybe what I did was still wrong, and I am justifying everything to myself, but the results don't lie. My team is safer now than they ever have been. And I am home. I watch the sun bounce off Altair's tufts of black, curling hair and browse my computer for new, terrestrial, jobs. Altair starts crying. I turn towards her and smile. I take her in my arms and laugh. I smile across the room at Franklin. "Don't worry," I tell her, steeping in the sweetness of her voice. "I'm here."

See Spencer Nitkey's story "Calling Me Home" online at Metaphorosis.
If you liked it, leave a comment. Authors love that!
Remember to subscribe to our e-mail updates so you'll know when new stories are posted.

About the story

This story came to me after an afternoon reading articles about quantum mechanics. Immediately I became obsessed with the idea of quantum entanglement, the fact that you can, essentially "entangle" two particles, so that, even when they are separated, moving one, affects the other. Recently, in 2017, a team of Chinese researchers tested the limits of entanglement by sending one entangled particle up in a satellite, 1200 kilometers from the other. The two particles were still entangled! I read that Einstein had called quantum entanglement "spooky motion at a distance". Anything that can make a scientist use the word spooky seems like perfect science-fiction fodder to me. Consciousness is a perpetual interest of mine, and eventually the idea of what a synthesis of consciousness and quantum entanglement could mean formed the conceit of this story.

Then the real work of writing began. I started by trying to find a central character. Claire came to me pretty quickly. I recently started a new job (which I love), but it made me think about how hard it can be to juggle life and work, even under the best of circumstances. What would it look like if a company, using science, had control over the physical location of your consciousness? What would it be like trying to start a family on Earth while working on the other side of the solar system? These questions formed the basis of the story and the rest followed.

A question for the author

Q: Do you use critique groups or other resources to polish your writing?

A: I love using critique groups. I was lucky to have the chance to study creative writing in college, and the opportunity to learn from a couple of really incredible professional writers and participate regularly in workshops and learn from my peers was something I took for granted until after I graduated. Now, I have a small writing group I attend semi-regularly. I am also grateful that my fiancée is almost as excellent an editor as she is a writer. She's been my first reader for years, and when I'm smart enough to follow her advice, my stories always come out better. I think, especially with speculative fiction, it's important to have beta-readers and critiques. I often have a clear idea of the world and conceit of a story, but I can't always tell how clearly that is being communicated with a reader until I've had the chance to hear from someone. Feedback is how we grow and improve, and I'm thankful for all the groups and people who have helped me improve.

About the author

Spencer Nitkey is a speculative writer, a researcher, and an educator who lives in New Jersey. His first intellectual love was nuclear physics and his second love was poetry. Science Fiction has been a happy median between those two. Now, when he's not busy dancing in the kitchen with his fiancée, dreaming about planting chestnut trees, or slowly reading *Gravity's Rainbow*, he's probably writing and imagining futures, presents, and pasts.

Devilish Calliope and the Ungrooviest Apocalypse

Evan Marcroft

I'd just worked the handcuffs loose when my phone started vibrating in my pocket. Even hanging by my ankles above impending doom, I knew I'd be in *real* shit if I didn't pick up. I made a sort of cup out of my hand and pressed the phone to my ear. "This is Devilish urgently speaking."

"Devilish. It's me. Are you free to talk?"

I glanced up, or rather down, into the flame-rimmed iris over which I'd been suspended by my ankles. Through a shimmering of superheated spacetime, the stratified circles of Hell were bared like flayed muscle. The radioactive unlight of hellfire brought tears to my eyes, and not for the first time I wished I'd packed a thing of Visine. I always think I won't need it, and I always do. "Very briefly," I said.

"You were supposed to report in yesterday," K.K. continued, audibly irate. "I hear chanting. Are you still working on the Alchemist Affair?"

I was, and things were starting to get real un-groovy, by my professional estimation. The man in question stood outside the chalk pentagram that kept the wound between dimensions from hemorrhaging into our reality. Each word in his black tome was written in the blood of a virgin sacrifice, and with every utterance that wriggled many-legged from his lips, his portal punched deeper into the damned-digesting guts of Gehenna, towards the entity the Alchemist sought to unleash. When at last it slouched into the world, suffice to say the general grooviness of Southern Germany would tank like stock in VHS.

Things were going well enough for the Alchemist that he could pause his recitation to shake his fist at me and crow, "Call for all the help you like, Devilish Calliope! Nothing can stop me now!" His coterie of disciples and colleagues and groupies cackled unctuously from the wings. I recognized a couple of famous novelists, two Nobel laureates, and an Olympic curler—all nude, as a matter of course. It was the latter who'd caught me snooping through the castle's dungeons and brained me with a corn broom. I could see how she'd won gold.

"Yeah well," I grumbled, "you know how it goes. One minute you're doing so and so, and the next it's all crazy, and then whatever happens. Bing bang boom. It's a whole thing."

"A whole thing."

I was sure I had a better answer somewhere, but right then my skull was too packed with blood to fit long thoughts. "Yes ma'am."

I detected screams in the static of her pause. Necromagnetic interference from the pit below. "Be that as it may, I have another thing I'm sure you'll find even more whole. A Condition: Critical, to be precise."

"You know," I heard the Alchemist mutter to an adjunct goon, *"I didn't want to say it, but this is just slaughtering the mood."*

A Condition: Critical. Now that was interesting. This thing with the Alchemist was a Condition: Convenient for comparison, which meant that it was not literally or figuratively the end of the world. A couple million dead, tops. I was only here because I wasn't busy with something else. "No shit," I said.

"Finish up there and come into the office. We've got a ticking clock situation."

"Don't worry about me. I'll be okay."

"I said come into the office," she snapped, and hung up.

"Finally," the Alchemist groused. "Do you text during movies too?"

"I'm done," I said, and hucked my phone at his head.

It was a good hit, got him right in the eye. The Alchemist yelped like a cartoon dog, stumbled over his curly-toed slippers and across the pentagonal firewall between realities, which instantly reduced him to a shrieking skeleton. In MESSIARC, we called that a bank shot. Things got out of hand fast. Stygian flames raced along the Alchemist's bones, and his goons went up like oily rags as the chamber became an inferno. Suspended a hundred feet in the air, I was spared for the moment, but with heat's propensity to rise, that moment wouldn't last. I lunged one way and then the other, setting myself to swinging like a pendulum. At the height of my arc, the rope around my ankles snapped off its hook and hurled me face-first through a window. Fortunately for me this had gone down in an old Bohemian palace; something more OSHA-compliant and I'd have been screwed. Unfortunately for me, on the other side of the window was a hundred-foot drop to a cobblestone courtyard. My teeth broke my fall, and I wound up a flattened Coke-can full of broken glass.

"Ow," I said, and also, "fuck."

But the immortality clause in my contract wouldn't let me die without a better excuse, and so I had to sit there and twiddle my metaphorical thumbs while my pulverized bones figured themselves out. There was a time I'd have been glad to be alive. I remembered that waterslide rush of improbable survival, how it jumpstarted my senses and made the world feel new again. But when you felt that day after day, you got numb to it. Started to dread the figurative plunge and welcome the towel-off afterwards.

I'd saved the world this time, I'd have to do it again tomorrow, and I'd probably get screwed on overtime, though honestly that was on me. I'd signed up for the forces of Infinite Good, not Infinite Benefits. No, these days all I looked forward to was a motel shower and a nap afterwards. One had to make do with the many small ends of things.

"This is possibly the direst assignment of your career," K.K. said. "Do you mind if I swear for emphasis?"

"Permission granted."

Her six arms made anxious gestures. All three of her faces spoke in tandem. "*You can't afford to fuck this up.*"

Back in the day, Kalamkari Kannon had been one of MESSIARC's best operatives, fighting for harmony across this iteration of Earth under deific guise, until the Higher-Ups promoted her into administration, where her prodigious skills were mostly useless. Her days were now spent making sure jerks like me did our jobs worse than she ever had. I did that better than anyone.

"Well, now I feel like I have to," I said.

I watched a universal truth drift blithely past her window, harassed by a shoal of profound revelations. K.K's office floated in a lower layer of Nirvana, a state of existence reachable only from a degree of enlightenment. Monks of all faiths spent decades in chaste meditation to forget their flesh. I'd gotten here through an unholy concoction of Angel Dust, peyote, and *Psilocybe azurescens* that I called the Conference Call, and which could make cockroaches see god. My body was currently comatose in a Motel 6 south of Reno. I admired my astral self in the back of K.K.'s laptop. Still looking sharp, I had to say.

"So, what's it this time?" I asked. "Moon vampires? Nazi ghosts? Permutations thereof?"

"You wish it were those common things," K.K. scoffed. "Vercingetorix Smooth has resurfaced."

I froze mid-ogle, an ambushed Narcissus. "Shit. When?"

"This morning. At eleven hundred hours, the—"

"He's gone over to MEGAVILE," I cut in. "Hasn't he?"

"It appears so."

My throat got tight and my neck got itchy, the way they do when you swallow too much at once, or see a bear coming at you with a loose brick in hand. You live as long as I have, you find the body only has so many responses for discomfiting things. "Great," I managed. "Groovy."

I'd known, from the day he'd run off, that Smooth would turn up again eventually. The guy had been on the front lines longer than anyone, K.K. included. He wouldn't go get himself killed off-screen like some side character. The question had been which side would claim him. In the eternal dodgeball game between multiversal good and multiversal evil, nobody didn't get picked. I'd hoped, futilely I suppose, that he'd find his way back to MESSIARC. He still owed me for bagels.

"What did he do?"

K.K. tapped a button and her projector flickered on. "This is need-to-know information. I wish you did not need to know, but God help us, you do. At eleven-hundred hours this morning, MESSIARC's Department of Inadvisable Science was attacked by the transuniversal terrorist unit called the Wild Hunt—a known branch of MEGAVILE. They were led by Vercingetorix Smooth."

She tapped another button, and a grainy surveillance still appeared. A squadron of motorcycles hauled fiery ass across the ginger sands of Mars, leaving a concrete fortress shattered in their rear-view mirrors. These weren't your slippery-sleek Kawasaki ninjamobiles. These were burly, chrome-bellied *choppers*, and there was no mistaking the figure who rode at their head, looking like a devil on wheels in his shiny new leather duds.

Good to see you, bud.

"We lost six operatives repelling their assault," K.K. went on, "and we could not prevent Smooth from absconding with a prototypical kaleidoquantumly correlated thermonuclear device."

I frowned at that, momentarily perplexed. "A kaleidoquantum... Oh god, no. Really? We made a Voodoo Nuke?"

K.K. sighed for about a minute straight. Three mouths, three times the lung capacity. "The Department of Inadvisable Science exists to preemptively innovate and isolate dangerous technologies. If we don't invent it, MEGAVILE will."

I took off my glasses and hung them from my collar. I did not need corrective lenses to see the looming mountain of irony. "You might say that was… inadvisable."

Two hands massaged K.K.'s temples while another worked a stress ball. The rest looked about ready to throttle me. "These decisions are not mine to make," she replied stiffly. "Anyway. The present danger cannot be overstated. If activated, the device will detonate every nuclear weapon within ten billion iterations of this universe. The death-toll will be incalculable. Misery and disorder will proliferate on an unprecedented scale. While the frontline of this conflict is ever in flux, the Higher-Ups have deemed this eventuality an unacceptable concession to MEGAVILE. Given your history with Operative Smooth, they believe that you are uniquely qualified to locate him and retrieve the device."

As the arbiter of all things groovy and not, I had to admit that an apocalypse to the zillionth power was decidedly ungroovy. "Who's to say he still has it?" I asked.

"If he'd handed it off to MEGAVILE, they'd have used it without hesitation.

He's holding on to it for reasons unknown and disconcerting." Three of her eyes drilled into me like they could torture out a hidden answer. The other three looked very tired. "*Do* you know where to find him?"

Did I know where to find a universe-hopping biker assassin? It wasn't like he'd been sending me postcards from balmy Bora Bora. But him keeping the Voodoo Nuke? That got my mind a-whirring. Vercingetorix Smooth had a reason for everything. What I knew, perhaps better than anyone, was that it was never the reason you suspected. "Not a clue," I said. "But give me a deadline to run up against and I'm sure I'll panic into something."

"The deadline is whenever your ex-partner decides to use the damned thing," K.K. replied. "You'll know when you reach it."

Thirty-two hours hence, I was cruising up the I-90 towards the heart of Chicago. The city rose ahead of me like a large urban conglomeration. To my right, Lake Michigan was a big blue thing. The come-down from enlightenment had pretty much depleted my capacity for abstraction.

Initially, I'd had no idea where to start looking for Smooth. K.K. hadn't been a whole heaping of help either. Agents were being mobilized across all realities, what with the transuniversal threat. Given the emergency, I figured I'd be given a crack team of my Earth's best operatives to work with, but one apocalypse did not put others on hold.

"Busy day?" I'd asked, to which she'd swiveled her monitor to show me a werewolf eating the president.

"Busy millennia."

But I'd remembered that the Wild Hunt had been active for centuries before Smooth took over. They'd made plenty of appearances from this Earth, pillaging, slaughtering, and recruiting from among its most brutal souls. A dip into my pool of snitches had given me a lead on a possible Wild Hunt rider operating out of the Windy City, and that had led me here, to the curb outside the old Biograph Theater, secret lair of one Professor Marcus Marchpane, mad scientist extraordinaire.

I found my way into the theater's secret basement without difficulty, fiddling with every doodad in the prop closet until a trapdoor opened beneath a box of wigs. I breezed impatiently through the various traps therein, the gases and the lasers. I didn't have time to indulge the mad professor's nonsense. I'd been through this routine a hundred times. I couldn't remember the last time I'd been surprised. Or made an impact, for that matter. The covert struggle between multiversal good and evil was trapped in perpetual stalemate. MESSIARC championing order, liberty, good vibes, and taxes filed on time, with MEGAVILE harbinging everything opposite: chaos, fascism, ska, and indiscriminate genocide. We'd win one battle, MEGAVILE the next. We'd stop an eruption, they'd shoot a duke. For every score, a counter-score, kicking the end further down the road. So it went, and so it would go, one side one-upping the other ad infinitum.

At least with TV you could turn the reruns off.

The lab under the trapdoor was crammed with your standard mad science shit. A tesla coil that spat lightning randomly. A thing that went splort in a tube. I subdued the proprietor with a masterfully executed Krav Maga Sleeper

Hold, which is what I call an ether-soaked rag, then laid the professor down on a pile of loose brains. It wasn't him I had questions for.

Death doesn't give warnings, but sometimes it steps on a twig. As I straightened up, the tell-tale crackle of negatronic particles ionizing reached my ear. I ducked, watched a ray of acidic light melt a hole in the cinderblock wall, and spun to see a blocky, 50's style robot charging another shot in its cannon-barreled forearm. On a well-oiled reflex, I swept a mirrored platter of medical tools off the gurney and threw it up like a shield before me; the killing beam struck it and rebounded, piercing the robot's steel chassis and carving it neatly in half across its knob-studded torso.

I knew better than to think that it was harmless in two pieces. I strode over and crumpled its gun barrel beneath my heel. "Three times is not the charm," I said, unhooking a spray bottle from my belt and taking aim at the robot's exposed wires and gears. "This here is water and bleach, my claptrapitous amigo. It's how I buy answers."

"Fuck you, pig," the robot shot back in a crackly speak-and-spell growl.

In response I gave it a two-second blast to the guts, eliciting a howl of autotuned pain. "That's for wasting two seconds," I said, with more of a snarl than I'd intended. "I know you're with the Wild Hunt. Tell me how to find Vercingetorix Smooth and you'll leave here without sounding like a broken VCR. Good deal?"

The robot's lightbulbs dimmed in suspicion. "Why do you want to know?"

I tightened my finger on the spray bottle's trigger.

"Alright, alright," the robot relented. "Here's the deal. I got dumptrucked in that Mars thing, so I figured I'd take the weekend for repairs. Smooth said he and the boys would pick me up Wednesday night. We're supposed to rendezvous at this bar on the Texas border called the Baño del Diablo. There's a leyline convergence there, makes for a real smooth ride getting in and out of this dimension. If you're looking to ambush him, go nuts, but if I were you, I'd write a will first."

"There. Was that so hard?" I turned for the door and as I did, something sharp kissed me on the earlobe. I looked at myself in the platter, and damned if there wasn't a feathered dart dangling off it like a hippy's earring. "Motherfuck!" I swore, rounding on the robot. I stomped down on its free hand until I snapped off its wrist. "I am in no mood, okay? Why does it always have to come to this? Why can't you MEGAVILE assholes just give me a fucking break for once?"

Despite its damage, the robot laughed, a sound like a staticky transmission cutting in and out. "Oh man, I know you. You're Devilish Calliope. You're just like Smooth said you'd be. You used to be cool. Now you're a dick."

"I'm not a dick," I began, but having just literally kicked a guy while he was down, I didn't have much of a follow-up. My anger went swirling down the drain, depositing a scum of tired shame on the toilet bowl of my soul. What was I getting worked up for anyway? I was basically unkillable; a poisoned dart would only make me puke and trip balls. The me that Smooth knew would have made a weekend out of that.

"Whatever," I muttered. "How does he know?" The last time I'd seen Smooth, there had been enough Beatles to solve a bridge and torch problem.

The robot shrugged its stumps. "Because you didn't quit like he did."

The last time I'd seen Vercingetorix Smooth, the year was 1974. What a time to have an immortal immune system. The Bee Gees were staying alive, Patty Hearst was making new friends, and Madagascar became the first country to recognize the Sahrawi Arab Democratic Republic. A landmark year across the board. Pants could be more than one color, your hair could wear its hair down, and life was good. But like Richard Nixon's sterling political career, all amazing things had to end.

Smooth and I had just clambered from the steaming debris of a Martian voidcruiser, whose prow had plowed a miles-long trench across New Mexico. I remember being drenched in liquified alien viscera and smelling like the locker room at Area 51, my once unimpeachable perm now gore-slicked and as impeachable as the president. We parked our coccyges on an aetherodynamic spoiler so that we could air-dry in the twilight, decompress, and watch the shadows stretch out long and blue across the desert.

"I've got a question," said Smooth.

"Is it *why did you press the red button and not the green one*?"

"No," he laughed, because he knew I did screwy shit to keep things interesting. "What does your life look like? Like, if you had to pick a physical thing, what would it be?"

That was a very 70's sort of question, very in vogue in the dynasty of horoscopes and LSD. A decade later, and the only answer you'd get would be *a big pile of cocaine*. As out of hand as the Mars assignment had gotten, I was already looking forward to the next. The build-up, the big plunge, the heart-stopping velocity towards the splashy mess at the bottom. Hell yeah. "A waterpark," I finally decided. "Where there're new slides all the time."

"That's funny. When I look at my life, I see a shelf full of books."

"Like *your* shelf, or a bookstore?"

"Irrelevant to the metaphor. My life is all these books in a series. *The Far-Out Case Files of Vercingetorix Smooth.* They look like a wild romp at first, and maybe the first one is, but not the first ten. You keep reading until you realize they're all the same beneath the cover, just with the names and places changed up like Mad Libs. The same ups and downs, the same stale tropes. And there're sixty-five million more to go. Would you want to keep reading? I don't know why I would."

I didn't know then, but that New Mexican twilight was a Rorschach blot. I recall that I'd seen the faintest seam of color on the horizon. The promise of a crisp morning and a fresh escapade. I would only realize later, over a sack of untouched bagels, that Smooth hadn't seen anything.

"The hero's journey is meant to be a circle," he murmured. "All I see ahead is a straight line."

"I think it's hard to think happy thoughts when you're covered in proof of life on Mars."

"Maybe, D."

"I say sleep on it," I said, which, in hindsight, is the most awful thing you can say to a conflicted friend. I could have offered to hold some of what he was carrying. I could have cracked a joke and laughed his trouble away. Instead, I'd told him to take it to a bed, where it would grow sour beneath the sheets, like a body in the throes of addiction. "You'll feel better tomorrow." *Deal with it yourself in a darkened room where you won't bother anybody. I'm sure you'll be alright.*

"Yeah probably." Smooth stood, teetering on the space-fin from another world. "Do me a huge. Tell K.K. I'm taking a personal day. I think I've earned it. I'll be back in on Wednesday. See you then, yeah?"

I remember being confident, as he sauntered off, that I *would* see him that Wednesday. I'd bring a bag of bagels to share, one with each kind of topping, because the Everything Bagel was still years from being obvious. And when he wasn't there that morning, I remember being pissed, more than anything, that I'd blown five bucks to watch bread go stale. It wasn't fair.

Things should have to say goodbye when they leave you.

The bar the robot had mentioned was a crumb of Vegas out there on the desert. Some enterprising scumbag had taken an old barn and slathered it in neon, put a couple of shitty picnic tables out front, a sign by the highway. I stumbled inside beneath a neon devil on a neon toilet, through a swamp fog of up-chucked beer and bad marijuana. Speakers on an empty stage were blaring White Rabbit, number one on my Top Ten songs to slowly fade away to. An enticing prospect, but I'd have to settle for getting sloppy. I groped my way to a barstool and collapsed, grateful for a seat that didn't kick me awake with every pothole.

"Howdy, stranger. What do they call you?"

I looked up. The girl behind the counter was maybe twenty, with a tattoo of a rose on her bicep, a week's worth of luggage under each eye, and a bruise on her jaw. Her smile had no business being kind, but it was anyway. "Devilish Calliope," I said. "You?"

"Mona. What kind of name is that? Greek?"

"It's a code name," I shrugged. "I'm sort of a secret agent."

"Nice to meet you, mister secret agent." That warm smile again. She seemed to mean it. What a welcome thing to find out here in nowhere. "How do you like your martinis?"

"In my belly."

I took whatever she gave me without looking and threw it at my tonsils. Mona looked concerned at this. "That there's money in the bank and I'm still worried. Want to share your woes, stranger?"

"Who says I got woes?"

Mona shrugged. "Wouldn't be here if you didn't."

I actually could argue, having wound up in worse places under happier circumstances—more than one birthday of mine had ended in a volcano—but she was right that I wouldn't pick this place over Seaworld.

I handed over my empty glass. Whatever it was hit my brain a second later and punched a hole through it. "Do people come in here and spill crazy personal shit on you a lot?"

"It's pretty much my whole job," she said.

She'd been warned. "Better than *my* job," I muttered. "I didn't put it together until I got down here, but this marriage has soured. I mean really, the kids are gone, and we're in separate beds. The thing is, they tell you that this is the most important thing you'll ever do, right? And yeah, I'm out there saving the world every day. But it never *stays* saved. For every bad guy I put away, there's three more on the waitlist for his doom castle. It's ridiculous."

I was surprised by the heat in my throat. This was more than I'd felt dangling over the Alchemist's hellhole. More than I'd felt in a long while. Maybe I needed a therapist. That or a larger tab. "Come on now, get it all out," Mona said. She poured me another anonymous drink, and I gave the one in my guts a friend.

"A co-worker once said this life was like reading the same story over and over again," I continued. "I didn't listen then, but he was right. And it gets old. Every go-through, every day you save, you lose a little crumb of enthusiasm, and when you run out, all that's left is a big asshole. That's me. Hi."

"Hi," Mona replied, unsure whether to laugh or frown.

I sighed, and smeared the sweat on my brow into my hair. "It feels... it feels like a race between finally doing something halfway consequential and just giving up. At this point, I don't know which one I'm rooting for."

"If you don't mind me saying," Mona said, "that sounds better than doing something that definitely doesn't matter." She was polishing a highball without looking at it. A dozen more were lined up along the countertop. I blinked, and saw the bar through her eyes. It went much further than I knew, snaking years into the past and decades into her future.

"Been working here long?" I asked.

She smirked. "You know any other shitty desert bars hiring?"

I had to admire a lady who could push a lot of hurt down with a cheek muscle. "Listen," I said. "I was serious about the whole secret agent thing. I've got bad guys showing up any minute, and it's going to be a whole thing. Do yourself a favor and clear out while you can."

Mona shrugged, like this was every day for her. "Thank you kindly, but I got rent to pay. I don't get to be scared of much. You and your pals just pay for anything you break, 'kay?"

I was about to elaborate when life interrupted like the asshole it was. Every head not face-down in vomit turned as the stealthiest storm I'd ever heard cleared its throat. Lightning flogged the Earth in a dozen places, and the thunder that followed sounded like unmuffled engines. Headlights knifed through the mazarine twilight. One by one, a squadron of motorcycles skidded to a stop in a barricade outside the bar and let off a procession of monstrosities. Octofiends from Planet Zed; vampire honnies with gold-capped fangs; extradimensional entities of such weird physics that my eyes could perceive only their spurs and bandannas. Their collective rap sheet would have killed a rainforest. The Wild Hunt, ride or die.

They sauntered in, silent as pallbearers, and stood aside to let barflies take wing. The glass in Mona's hands shattered on the floor as their leader filled the doorway and crouched to squeeze inside. At full height his snout clipped the rafters; his feet stamped three-clawed craters in the floor. Mona sucked in a breath, as if she'd never seen a forty-foot Tyrannosaurus Rex in a biker jacket stomp into a bar.

Like I said, the guy had been on the job longer than anyone.

"Hi, Smooth," I said.

"Hi, D," said Vercingetorix Smooth. "Happy Wednesday."

My old partner settled his sixteen scalebound tons down beside me at the bar, his massive skull casting me in shadow, his tail curling around my stool. A telescoping robotic claw dropped a crinkled ten on the counter. To her credit,

Mona had bravely stayed put, and began to fill a mug.

"You look like you need an adrenalin shot," Smooth remarked.

"You look extinct," I replied. "You knew I'd be here."

"No other reason to gank a Voodoo Nuke. Other than the obvious one, I mean." He snapped a prosthetic finger, and a betentacled crony placed a locked briefcase on the counter between us. "I wanted to see you again," he said. "It's not easy to hang out, the way things are. I thought, 'those assholes must be running 'ol Devilish ragged. I'd better touch base.' But how, I wondered, to get him alone without everyone freaking out?"

I glanced casually at the innocuous case, and beat down the urge to run screaming from it. "The Voodoo Nuke. I called it that too."

Smooth had no lips, but I'd learned to tell when he was smiling. "I bet you did."

"I can't let you leave with that thing," I said.

"That sucks," he replied. "Normally you could have it, but the boss is on my ass about this one. I'm afraid I've got to be inflexible. How about you put it out of your mind? Let the inevitable come to pass. Tell me how you're getting on."

I swiveled my stool to look him in the eye. I picked the left one, it being the only one I could see. "This is what I'll tell you. I've got a company card, you've got the spoils of a thousand worlds. We're at a bar, and we've both come a long way. We'll drink for it. I win, you hand it over, and go back to revving your engines in quiet neighborhoods like the villain you are."

"*We'll drink for it,*" Smooth echoed bemusedly. "What do I get if I win?"

"If you win, you get me."

Smooth lapsed into a silence that bordered on theatrical. I waited without a doubt he'd go for it. Not because he craved another servant of evil, no. Because he missed me. I knew that because I *was* his friend, and I wanted the same thing.

I missed my buddy.

Smooth affixed a slit pupil on Mona, and downed his mug in one pull, letting the suds dribble between his fangs. Hops comingled with gut-fermenting carrion, became something even I wouldn't huff.

"Line 'em up."

Mona looked at him, then me. "Are you really the good guy?"

"The goodest here," I said in full honesty.

"And that box is dangerous."

I pinched an invisible grain of rice. "Little bit."

She nodded at the ground and set her jaw. "Alright. Hoo boy."

Smooth had a crossroads devil who could whip up a magically binding contract. Neither of us would be wiggling out. With everything signed in blood, the drinking commenced. Mona poured shots and we downed what we were given. Vodka, gin, other pellucid poisons. My kidneys had survived tours of Australia, Russia, and Arizona U, but Smooth was a gigantic dinosaur, so who could know the odds? It was cordial, at first, drinking as we caught up on the last few decades. He didn't seem to mind me foiling MEGAVILE's plots, and I guiltily enjoyed hearing about the interesting people he'd been eating. We could have gone on into the morning. But it was only a matter of time before we found that unavoidable question at the bottom of a glass. Best to rip the band-aid off.

"Why did you quit?" I asked.

Smooth handed Mona his latest empty and took a refill. "It's like I said in the desert." He'd barely begun to slur his words. Meanwhile I felt like the barn had left port, and the seas were getting choppy. "The danger, the adventure, the intrigue—it lost its edge. I ran out of new things to see. Reasons to keep going. And you know what? It never got results. Nothing changed. Nothing got better. At least not for long. Eventually I had to ask myself: what's the point of playing a game you can't win?"

"Like you can win over at MEGAVILE either," I snorted.

"That's where you're wrong," he said, and my heart, which had been chugging along just fine, lurched down a dark sideroad.

"Here's the truth that MESSIARC will never tell you. Nobody can *really* win this thing. Not me, not you. They hold evil up like something we can all stop if we hold hands and sing *We Are The World*, but it's not. Evil, it turns out, is not an outcome. It is a process. Its goal isn't to stamp out good forever. No. All it wants is to *be*. To exist, perpetually in flux, waxing and waning. Letting hope flourish just to be crushed, ad infinitum. Think about it. A slasher must hide between murders so everyone can hope he's gone. A tyranny must fall so that it can rise under a new flag and conquer again, just as a forest burns and grows anew. If evil *actually* won, if every last scrap of happiness were gouged out of every universe, it would be left with *nothing to do.*"

The clap of his glass on the countertop went through my booze-bruised brain like a shockwave. "Evil doesn't want a knock-out," he said. "Evil wants to exist. And it always will, because evil is what good must inevitably become." Smooth sent another shot nonchalantly down the hatch. I'd almost forgotten the one in my own hand.

"Don't believe me?" Smooth replied to my silence. "Hello, I'm the proof. Epochs on the job and still I fell. Lucifer did it for less, and sooner. The best of intentions still break down, when the going gets rough, when the going never ends. Systems corrupt. Wills erode. Agents defect. It's not about choosing to do bad; that's hard. It's about admitting how pointless it is to be good, which is easy. It's leaning into the wind that's blowing and letting it take you where you're already bound to go. Don't tell me you haven't felt it pushing. Sooner or later, the decay of decency claims all."

He turned to baste me in a cloud of yeasty gizzard-stink, as revolting as it was painfully nostalgic. "The end that you're holding out for isn't coming. Tumbling forever between saved and unsaved, the world is a tossed coin that cannot fall. There is no win-condition for you, only the monotony, the score and the counter-score. And I'll tell you what, my friend: if our team can't lose, well, *that's enough like winning for me.*"

He protracted a claw and gently clapped my shoulder. "Come on, man. Join me already. This Wild Hunt thing? Fuck it. Out that door is a multiverse of other shit to do. We'll kick around infinity and do whatever, just you and me, and it'll feel *good, because that's what evil is.* Freedom from hope, freedom from *giving a shit.* Throw this thing, and we can drink to celebrate your liberation instead."

I stared at the droplets of vodka trickling down the inside of my glass, bitter liquor fast becoming sticky dregs to be washed out and replaced.

Was Smooth right? Hell if I knew for sure. But like all forked-tongued lawyers, he spoke himself a good case. Everything, in my experience, only got worse. Even the immortal decayed. Just look at me: I used to be a priest. He didn't need to tell me that every bit of good I'd ever done was doomed to be undone. I knew what Eve felt when she saw that sweet apple hanging there. The serpent had been surplus. Something so simple sold itself. For her, potassium. For me, a release.

From hope. From care.

Maybe it didn't matter whether he was right. If some final triumph over evil was coming, it was too far in the future even for an immortal to see. However long my life was, it was all I could worry about. No matter what, I'd be spinning in circles until something killed me; I didn't have to be spinning alone. Yeah, I'd have to learn how to ride a motorcycle and commit unspeakable atrocities, but both those things would become second-nature in time. The game would never let me go, no, but at least—

At least I could play with a friend.

Swaying, I groped at the counter. One more drink. This one to numb the choice.

I sipped the next shot through my teeth. I froze as the taste struck my tongue.

My eyes searched for Mona's, and she looked pointedly elsewhere.

I thought. And then I grinned.

"You almost had me," I said. "But I know something you don't."

Smooth's scaly brow crinkled. "I can't understand you. You're slurring."

Yeah I was, so never mind. I slugged the shot down and waved for another.

Smooth and I went back and forth, shot for shot, in silence now, his play made and answered. I stared him down, teetering only slightly, as his eyelids began to droop, his tail slashing herky-jerkily across the floor. Seeing me remain impossibly upright seemed to galvanize him. He began to drink faster, as if to prove he could. His side of the bar quickly grew cluttered with glass. I drank and waited. The night crunched down on us, a shrinking prison.

Shot number thirty-two hovered between Smooth's jaws. The Wild Hunt held its collective breath. Behind the bar, Mona edged away. A dollop dropped onto his tongue. Then two. Finally he dropped the glass down his throat and swallowed it whole. Gave his teeth a mocking lick.

"Give me another," he triumphantly declared.

And then his mass tilted sideways and crushed me flat.

The Wild Hunt took off not long after. I wasn't sure how they'd got Smooth out; the place was empty when I finished regenerating apart from Mona, who'd presumably watched it happen with the same expression of fascinated horror. They'd left the suitcase on the un-crushed half of the counter, as per the unbreakable deal.

"I won't be able to sleep without seeing that," Mona said.

"Try feeling it." The transformation from pancake to man had wrung the liquor out of me. "That was a real dangerous thing you did. Hell if it didn't work though." She'd had a final shot lined up for me. I drank it now, needing the fluids. Pure, unfiltered water, straight from the tap.

"You looked like you needed it." Mona shrugged like it was nothing. Even so, she wore that wide-eyed, shellshocked expression you get from your first blast of weird. No, it would not wear off in time. It was pretty much her face now.

"Yeah, kinda," I admitted. "You got a pen?"

She did, and I took a minute to scratch out a number on a gently-used napkin. "Hold on to this. It's for a lady named K.K. If she doesn't pick up the first time, leave her fifty messages."

Mona frowned, but took it anyway. "I don't get it."

"You saved the world today," I replied. "You looked death in the face while you cheated it. That's a solid resume, supposing you're looking to make a career change. If you do call, tell her Devilish sent you." Not that it would be a sterling reference.

She nodded, and put the napkin in her pocket. "Sure," she said. I couldn't tell what she meant by that, but I knew what I'd bet if I had to.

I stepped outside with the briefcase to find that someone had slashed the tires on my Matador, lowering its value not one cent. I put the Voodoo Nuke under the seat and sat on the hood to make a call. The Wild Hunt had taken the storm with them; the stars winked overhead like a million proud uncles.

"Operative Calliope." K.K. sounded her usual, harried self. "What is it? What's going on?"

"Nothing," I said. "I got the thing."

"I... what?"

"I got it," I said again, gently. "I met Smooth, got the bomb, sent him packing. It's alright now. You don't have to worry. Everything is groovy. Take a rest."

Silence on the other end, but I could hear her unclenching, breathing out, for the first time all day. Maybe for the first time all year.

"Thank you, D," she sighed. "I'm glad to hear that. And I will."

I smiled for no one's benefit. "Hey, so what's next? Where do you need me now?"

But she didn't need me anywhere, it turned out. The stars had aligned. For at least this effervescent moment, the world was out of crises.

My next call was for a tow. Afterwards, I stretched out against my windshield, closed my eyes, and felt the Earth glide through space, a ship on calm seas. I wished I could have told Smooth what I'd realized in the bar. Twice now I'd stayed silent when I shouldn't have. *Evil is what good must inevitably become.* He was spot-on there. But what I'd figured out was that, emergent from unlikely places, unexpected faces, good sprang from nowhere at all. For every me that lost faith on the slog towards nowhere, there was a

Mona. When you framed it like that, good was infinite too.

Maybe I'd mention it when next he came around. I doubted this'd be the last time. The night could not stay quiet forever. The universe was too in love with disarray; it would never be finally alright. But Smooth's logic had been compelling. If evil's continuance was its objective, then it held that any dent in that continuity was a victory. There could be no great ending to things, but if I busted my ass for it, I might find a little conclusion here and there, like this one, the twilit calm between the end of one book and the cover of another, in which the world felt safe to do something beautiful like simply chill, and that felt enough like winning to me.

Fleeting, but not nothing, the many small ends of things.

See Evan Marcroft's story "Devilish Calliope and the Ungrooviest Apocalypse" online at Metaphorosis.
If you liked it, leave a comment. Authors love that!

Remember to subscribe to our e-mail updates so you'll know when new stories are posted.

About the story

I've always been a fan of the ongoing fantasy/sci fi series. Your *Dresden Files* in particular, and anything by Simon R. Green. I would devour every new installment as soon as it came out and wait impatiently for the next one. As I developed into a writer myself, however, and grew a more critical eye, I noticed that as book heaped upon book, as characters changed sides, died, and resurrected, as plot-lines grew ever more entangled, that I never seemed to reach the ends of these sagas, and see how everything ultimately shook out. I found myself wondering how these eternally cocksure and self-deprecating characters would react if they could step outside their stories and see just how much further they had to go before they could rest at last. This story was born from that pity. It's the message I could send to my favorite protagonists, if I could. Things might never be finally alright, but that's no reason to give up.

A question for the author

Q: What happens when you hit writer's block head on?

A: When I hit writer's block head on, I usually realize that what I'm writing is boring. Not the entire story necessarily, but typically an event in that story, which is playing out too straightforwardly to spark my interest, a scene of transportation from one location to another, for example. I find that my writing surges when I'm describing something unusual, or depicting something commonplace from an uncommon angle. If I'm finding it hard to proceed, my go-to trick is to make it harder for myself. Rather than drive us to the new location from our protagonist's perspective, I can hop into the perspective of a bird watching our hero drive through the narrow streets below, or from the point of view of the city beneath him, wincing as he steers his car through the folds of its asphalt brain. Sometimes the smoothest route towards what I want to accomplish is the more roundabout one.

About the author

Evan Marcroft is a speculative fiction writer from California currently residing in Chicago with his wife. Evan uses his expensive degree in literary criticism to do menial data entry, and dreams of writing for video games, but will settle for literature instead. His works of science fiction, fantasy, and spine-curdling horror can be found in a variety of venues across the internet, such as *Strange Horizons*, *Asimov's*, and multiple times in *Metaphorosis*.

evan-marcroft.squarespace.com, @Evan_Marcroft

All That Remains

Michael Gardner

The boy doesn't have a name, but Father calls him Progeny. He was born underground, and grew up in near darkness. In the tunnels. Walking the spaces between compact earthen walls, buttressed intermittently with wooden beams, glow worms the only luminescence.

His eyes are good. He sees shapes where Father sees shadows. He sees shadows where Father sees nothing.

He walks now, very quietly. Now is the quiet time. It is a rule. He hunches to keep his head from grazing the ceiling, striding confidently along the well-worn trail, one hand held out, fingers skimming the gritty walls, now a beam, now earth, now a beam.

Abruptly, he emerges into an expansive cavern of dark rock. At the back of the cave is a deep, rock crevice—the pit, as Father calls it—where Progeny dumps the dirt from his excavations. Before the pit though, are pools. The pad of Progeny's footsteps on the hard surface echoes as he moves toward them. Water leaks from somewhere up high, running in rivulets down the far wall covered in yellow moss and white fungal protrusions, ending with a caress of the surface of the pond. The water gurgles and gulps—wet whispers floating around the cavern.

Progeny approaches the water. It smells fresh and sweet. He falls to his knees by the edge, staring into the depths, where he sees white lines criss-crossing beneath the dark surface. Eels. With a violent splash, Progeny snatches a large one from the pond with strong, practiced hands.

He grins as he bites into the writhing flesh, enjoying the saltiness of the blood.

When he is sated, he will retrace his steps through the tunnels to meet Father at the shelter. There, on hard wooden boards, he will receive his lessons.

Lessons after the mid-meal. Another rule.

Father stands in the middle of the shelter, watching Progeny approach. He is a short man, with white hair, and a back as straight as the wooden beams in the tunnels. Around his neck hangs a large key on a chain. Progeny knows it unlocks the storeroom, which houses towers of canned goods, jars of preserved fruits, drums of powdered milk and eggs.

Progeny stops at the edge of the shelter, and waits for Father's invitation to join him. It is a rule.

The shelter is a simple construction. A raised wooden platform, three walls and an earthen ceiling. The front of the shelter is open to the tunnels. The rear wall has a small hatch, through which Progeny must crawl when instructed. Father's bedroll is packed away neatly in a corner.

Father squints down at Progeny through the gloom. He removes a crank-powered flashlight from his ragged trousers, winds it, and points the flickering beam at Progeny's face. Progeny squeezes his eyes shut against the pain, then turns away until Father directs the light elsewhere. Hesitantly, Progeny opens his smarting eyes and sees that Father has placed the torch, bulb down, on the floor of the shelter, a small wavering circle of light surrounding the device. Instead of the torch, Father now holds a strand of wire, three feet long. It is his teaching aid.

"Come. The lesson begins," Father says.

Progeny steps into the shelter, then kneels before Father. Progeny lowers his head, and his eyes, but opens his ears and mind as previously instructed. Father begins his oration.

Progeny has heard much of Father's speech before. There is little new these days. Father talks of the before, and the wickedness of the world. He talks of the righteous end. He mocks the unprepared. He talks of the remainder, the lesions, and the living rot. He talks of sinners receiving what was owed, and the joy of being saved.

As he talks, Father flicks the wire through the air to emphasise his points.

Father talks of Mother. Father remains confused about her. She was taken unfairly, he says with less vigour. He sounds perplexed, and sad. But he moves on. He talks about Progeny. He talks about burdens and disappointment.

Finally, when Progeny's knees ache, and his legs and feet tingle with numbness, Father finishes, places a hand on Progeny's head, and entwines his fingers in Progeny's fine hair.

"Time for your question, Progeny."

Progeny swallows, lets the silence build while he frames the question in his mind. He places both of his hands on top of Father's hand on his head.

"If the surface sickness has indeed cleansed the earth of sin," Progeny says, "why do we still need to hide in the tunnels?"

Progeny feels Father's hand twitch. Progeny swallows again, waiting. Just as he thinks Father will not answer, Father speaks.

"We do not hide in the tunnels, we live. The sinners are vanquished, but the remainder roam the surface still."

"But you have also said that the saved inherit the earth, and the fallen—"

Father delivers a powerful blow to the soft flesh of Progeny's armpit with the wire switch. Progeny feels the familiar pain—a sharp bite, then a burning. He stifles a yelp. Warm blood trickles down his side, but he resists the urge to let go of Father's hand. That would only bring more punishment.

"You've had your question," Father says coldly. Progeny sucks in air, but says nothing.

"Blessed are those left in the dark," Father says, and he slides his hand out from under Progeny's, allowing Progeny to lower his arms to his sides, careful not to agitate the fresh cut.

"You are permitted to leave and work on the new tunnel," Father says.

Blessed indeed, thinks Progeny.

Progeny's tunnel is at the opposite end to Father's shelter, closer to the pools, and the pit where dirt can be discarded. His work progresses slowly, but he has made progress. He is not as experienced as Father in tunnel construction, and it has taken time to learn how and where to buttress them. Learning is slow when Father refuses to demonstrate his techniques, and Progeny is only permitted one question at a time.

His tunnel is narrower than any of Father's. He digs it out slowly so it does not collapse. But he is proud of his work, and proud he is adding to the structure of their home.

It is only recently that Father allowed Progeny to engage in excavation. Perhaps Father thinks it is busy work. Another way to encourage Progeny to reflect on the soul and mind, where naturally thoughts go when hands are occupied. Or perhaps Father realises that with Progeny occupied, he can enjoy that much more solitude.

This might be closest to the truth, as Father has never visited Progeny's site, for which Progeny is grateful. Because what Father doesn't know is that Progeny is digging up.

The entrance to Progeny's tunnel is about a metre and a half square. The tunnel continues straight on into the earth for ten metres, and is buttressed with wooden beams that Father provides from the storeroom. Wooden beams are also piled up outside the entrance of the tunnel, waiting to be used. And there is a cone-shaped pile of dirt that Progeny has yet to relocate, along with an empty tin of peaches that smells syrupy.

After ten metres, Progeny's tunnel turns up at a forty five degree angle, then continues for nearly thirty more metres. Progeny has also buttressed that part of the tunnel with wooden beams. He has done this in six places.

To work in his tunnel, Progeny must duck. It is too small to stand erect. He's working now on his knees.

He uses a short pickaxe to worry free a large stone, which pops out and falls to the floor with a thud. Progeny drops the pick and grabs at the rock before it bumps into his legs. He eases the stone behind him, sliding it next to a large bucket half filled with dirt.

The tunnel smells of damp, loamy earth, freshly turned. Progeny likes the smell. It is the scent of progress. So much nicer than the acrid smell of old sweat that Father exudes.

Progeny takes hold of his pickaxe once more and raises it, poised to strike at the tunnel wall again. But that is when he hears a murmur, and he hesitates, arm tensed, muscles coiled, ready to unwind.

He frowns. It is quiet again now and he questions whether he did, indeed, hear anything at all. But he waits, just to be sure.

It comes again. A soft murmuring that resonates through and from the tunnel walls. A sound familiar and yet strange. It reminds Progeny of times when he has caught Father mumbling to himself. But the wall cannot mumble, or murmur. And yet...

Progeny lowers the pick to the ground, then presses his ear against the cool earth, feeling the grittiness of the dirt against the side of his face. The noise is gone. Perhaps temporarily, perhaps for good. Progeny waits. And waits. And just as he is about to give up, it comes again.

Quiet rolling eddies of sound. First they are high pitched, soft. Then a pause. After, the mumbling is a little louder, and deeper.

He pulls back as realisation dawns. Two voices. The ground is transmitting the soft sounds of a conversation between two people. Close enough to hear, but not close enough to understand.

Progeny swallows. And swallows again. He doesn't know what this means. Father has said many times that he and Progeny were saved, no one else. Only the remainder continue above. But the remainder are sick, barely human. They don't converse.

So if not the remainder, then who?

Progeny kneels on the wooden floor of the shelter, his aching legs complaining. Father's lecture is longer than usual. He's saying a lot without saying much. Progeny is tired of listening, and hurting, so he takes the risk, breaks the rule, and speaks out of turn.

"There are people living above us," Progeny says.

Father's rant ends mid-stream, his mouth gaping, his eyes wide with shock, and anger.

Progeny hurries on. "I've heard them talking. Who are they?"

Father stares at him for a long time, long enough for Progeny to wonder if Father has died on his feet. But then he blinks, speaks.

"Only the remainder live above. You must have mistaken their moans of pain for communication."

"They were talking," Progeny fires back. "You know, don't you? You haven't—"

But his accusation is interrupted by a blow from the wire. Progeny moans. Father swings again, hard. Progeny sucks in the pain, like inhaling foul air.

"The remainder are tricky, evil. They would tempt us to the surface to infect us. But we are strong, Progeny, we are strong. Have faith."

"Liar."

Father's face blooms with blood, his eyes narrow. And then he swings the switch—once, twice, three times. On the fourth, Progeny catches the wire in his hand and yanks it from Father's grip. He rises to his feet and raises the switch menacingly.

"You've made an error. There are people up there," he yells. "People like us, and yet we are down here. Why? What are you afraid of?"

Father puffs his chest out, stands more erect. "Progeny," he says, "you speak out of turn and you will submit to re-education."

Progeny narrows his eyes, maintaining the anger. The hand holding the wire quivers. He tenses, ready to punish Father, but then he hesitates, and in hesitation he is done. He sees the aged man before him. Progeny falters, and his hand lowers, his shoulders slump, his eyes turn downward, and he drops the switch to the floor with a clatter.

"Yes, Father," he says. He moves toward the small door at the back of the shelter, drops to his knees and crawls through.

The hatch leads out into another tunnel, but the floor of this one has iron rails that snake into the blackness like a forked tongue. On them sits an old, rusted hand car. Progeny knows that this part of his home was a mine, once. A mine for what, he doesn't know, and Father has never said.

Progeny sighs, steps up onto the car, and releases the brake. He takes hold of the heavy walking beam, and begins to pump it up and down, the hand car squealing loudly as it edges forward. A deeper darkness is soon the reward for his exertions.

Progeny knows this trip. He trusts the rails, and yet careering along the track has him on edge. The hand car moves fast, then faster. He feels air on his face, cooling the sweat that has beaded on his forehead. The squeaking wheels provide the soundtrack.

Eventually, a faint green glow appears ahead, then grows larger as the car races on. It is bright enough to make Progeny squint, but not so bright as to hurt his eyes like Father's torch.

Progeny engages the brake and slows the car, which screams in protest, before stopping below the circle of light. Above him, in a crevice in the ceiling, a colony of glow worms writhe. They cast just enough light to illuminate the walls of the tunnel on which Father has hung photographs.

The first is black and white, a wedding photo of Mother and Father. In it, they both look happy, young, and carefree.

Next is a photograph of Progeny's grandparents, also black and white. They were dead when Progeny was born, but Father has put the photo on the wall to remind Progeny of where he came from.

Next is the front page of a twenty year old newspaper, framed. "Mystery virus strikes down 1 in 4." The subheading says that medical researchers are working around the clock to develop a vaccine.

Next are photos of the blockades, police in riot gear, officials in hazmat suits, panicked citizens pushing up hard against them.

There are more newspaper articles. "Quarantine zones established across the country." "Armed forces enforce the quarantine." "No progress with a cure." Each is accompanied by grainy black and white photos, in which the people look more and more wretched, and frightened, and helpless.

There are also photographs of the tunnels, newer, but unmistakeably them. There is the store room, filled with goods, the cavern and pools, and one photograph of a narrow shaft going up, and up, and up toward the surface. That shaft doesn't exist now. Progeny has searched, and he is certain that Father collapsed it many years before.

Last, there is a photograph of Father standing alongside Mother, who is heavily pregnant. They look as wretched and lost as the people in the newspaper articles. They stand near the storage room in the underground shelter. Mother has a wound near her lip. Something that could be mistaken for a cold sore, except it is not. Progeny knows that.

Progeny releases the brake and pumps the walking beam once more. The car rolls away from the shrine of history. Darkness descends again, the air whistling around him.

Progeny's heart beats harder, and he can feel the steady pulse of blood pumping in his chest, up his neck, in his temples. His breathing comes fast, hard, ragged. He doesn't want to finish the re-education. He wants to turn back, but he doesn't. He is convinced Father would know, so he pushes on. Cutting through the darkness. Metal wheels on rails screaming.

Finally, the darkness morphs into gloom, and he swallows down the lump in his throat. He engages the brake again, and the car slows, then stops just before the end of the tunnel.

There, illuminated by light from another colony of glow worms, is a withered corpse tied to the wooden beams. Its head hangs limp against its chest, thin dirty hair covering the left side of its face. Of the right side, most of the flesh is gone. Instead, leathered skin hangs loose, a flash of white bone beneath a tear in the cheek. The clothes are tattered, and swim on the decayed remains. The corpse has been there so long it no longer reeks, but smells earthy, and of dust.

Progeny steps down from the car, approaches, then kneels before the corpse.

"Forgive me, Mother," he says quietly. "I lost my patience with Father again."

When Progeny arrives back at the shelter, he's tired and sore. His arms ache from pumping the walking beam. His mind is a darting eel, swirling from one side to the other. He desperately wants to return to his tunnel, and sleep.

He engages the brake, and stumbles down from the car onto bare earth. He drops to hands and knees, and crawls back through the hatch of the shelter hoping desperately that the final admonishment is short.

The shelter is empty.

He shifts onto his haunches, surveys the room. Empty.

"Father?" he calls out. Nothing.

He is assaulted by a brief surge of nausea.

He knows exactly where Father has gone.

At the entrance of his tunnel, Progeny crouches and peers inside. It is quiet. Most of his tools remain outside, although the pickaxe is missing.

"Hello," Progeny calls, the sound disappearing, then echoing back. "Father?"

He hears grunting, and in the distance sees wavering light. Progeny hunches low and moves along the flat part of the tunnel until he reaches the incline. Up ahead, he spies Father. He's holding the pickaxe in one hand, and shining the beam of his flashlight toward the end of the tunnel with the other.

Father turns abruptly, and directs the torch at Progeny who winces in pain and shields his eyes with his hands.

"You," Father snaps. Through narrow slits, Progeny sees Father marching toward him, head bent to avoid the low tunnel ceiling. "You would create a gateway for the damned into our sanctuary."

Father is close now, and still he keeps the painful light on Progeny's face. It feels like needles in his brain. Even after he shuts his eyes tight, the light gets in.

"I wanted to get closer, to listen," Progeny says.

"You were tempted. You are tempted, you ignorant child. I let you dig and you toss that dirt casually over your shoulder and into my face. Up is damned."

"But how do you know?"

"Because I lived it," Father hisses. "Because I saw the people struck down. So many evil people. And good people, like your mother. But I saved you, and yet you show no faith in me. You want proof? You want to tunnel out, become infected and as you lay dying, say, 'Yes, Father was right'?"

The light sputters, dies. Progeny doesn't hear Father cranking the torch again, so he opens his eyes slowly. Father's eyes sparkle with fury.

"It's been so long, Father. They might have stopped the—"

Father cuts him off by cracking him hard across the cheek with his flashlight. Progeny sees lights again, his ears ring, and he tastes copper in his mouth where he has bitten his tongue.

"I should never have left you on your own for so long." Father turns and moves awkwardly back up the tunnel. "You will cease tunnelling, and submit to further re-education."

The words are a punch to the guts. Progeny stumbles after Father, banging his head painfully on a beam before ducking lower and pushing on.

"You will meditate on faith," Father says as he reaches the last buttress and halts. Progeny stops too, just behind him. Father turns to address Progeny.

"You will once again come to recognise that hell waits in the open air, while sanctuary is provided by me, below."

Father turns and swings the pickaxe at the wall, lodging it behind the support beam.

"No," Progeny yells. Father levers hard, and the beam comes loose and clatters to the floor. It's followed by a burst of soil. Father swings again, and the point of the pickaxe wedges behind the ceiling support. More dirt falls as he jerks the handle. The ceiling bulges, dirt trickles, but the beam holds.

Father yanks the pickaxe out and pulls it back over his shoulder, coiled and ready to swing. But before he does, Progeny lunges. He takes hold of Father's arm, surprising himself. He fights for control, but Father's grip is tight. Father grunts, twists, pulls.

"You will release me, boy," he screams into Progeny's face, spittle hitting him between the eyes.

"No," Progeny says from between clenched teeth. "This is not your decision."

Father wrenches, then pushes hard. Progeny loses his balance. Father seizes on his momentary advantage and shoves Progeny again, slamming him into the broken wall of the tunnel. The wind rushes from Progeny, but he refuses to let go. Dirt streams from the ceiling into his eyes, but he blinks it away. Father is close, leaning into him. His face is red, veins pulsing across his forehead.

"You're just like her," he screams. "Just like your mother. She wouldn't listen. Just a few days more, she kept saying. A few days more. She had too much faith in the goodness of people. In their cleverness. Now look at her."

Progeny notices tears in Father's eyes. Shocked, he lets go, and Father stumbles backward, nearly trips, but manages to maintain his balance. He holds the pickaxe across his chest, breathing heavily. He eyes Progeny warily.

"I'm sorry, Father. But this is different."

Father sighs, and Progeny watches the anger leave him. He suddenly looks very old, very frail. He clears his throat. "You're all that I have left of her."

Father says nothing more, and Progeny doesn't know what to say. The silence builds as they watch each other. An uncomfortable, painful silence.

"I can't," Progeny eventually says. He speaks softly, slowly. "I can't be your memory of her. I need to see for myself."

Progeny watches his Father's eyes harden, his mouth tighten into a thin line. Father roars, turns, and swings the pickaxe hard at the ceiling. And before Progeny can issue a warning, Father is lost under an avalanche of dirt, wood, dust, and debris.

Progeny dives away from the implosion, down the incline, slamming hard onto the sloped floor. He covers his head with his arms. The din of destruction fills his ears. Dirt and rocks strike at his back and legs, fast at first, but then slower. And then the noise dies away to a whisper as dirt continues to trickle from the damaged ceiling.

Progeny opens his eyes, squints to see through the dust. He pushes himself up off the floor, and turns to find Father half buried. His eyes are closed, and he has a large gash across his forehead. Dark blood runs past his ear and drips onto the dirt floor, which sucks it up greedily.

Progeny feels weak. He's breathing hard, trying to still the panic. He moves closer, drops to his knees, a hand hovering over his Father, but he can't bring himself to touch him. "Father," he says.

The old man's eyes spring open. He coughs, and sprays a fine red mist into the air. His breath gurgles in his chest. His eyes find Progeny. They're wide, pained, scared. They move toward the broken ceiling.

It's then that Progeny notices the breeze. A zephyr of cool air that is foreign, and confusing. And on it is a sweet scent that Progeny has never smelled before.

Progeny follows Father's gaze up, and sees it. There's a hole in the tunnel. And it leads outside. He looks back at Father, wide-eyed.

"Close the tunnel," Father says. "Save us. Save yourself."

"But Father—"

"Promise me," he wheezes. Blood bubbles from his lips. "Promise me you will heed your Father. This is how you protect yourself."

But Progeny doesn't believe that. He hasn't for a long time. He can't close himself off like Father has. But he doesn't say that to Father.

"Yes, Father," he says instead. He finally allows his hand to rest on Father's chest, and then he waits. He waits until Father's harsh breathing slows, then stops. He waits until Father simply stares up at the hole in the ceiling, unmoving.

Progeny feels numb, but also a little lighter. Father was the only person he ever knew. And in his way, Progeny thinks Father did care for him. But it's also a relief to know that Father won't demand anything from Progeny ever again.

Progeny closes Father's eyes, rises to his feet, and climbs up the mound toward the opening.

The sky is unfathomable—black-grey, dotted with billions of lights that sting Progeny's eyes, but he can't stop staring.

He feels like he is floating upward. He feels free.

There are strange sounds everywhere. Trills, whistles, a dull roar from far away. The world smells like a thousand cans of opened peaches, but better.

Progeny stands on soft, damp grass, trees surrounding him, the broken entrance to the tunnels at his feet. Nearby is a bench, and a colourful construction that confuses Progeny. It has a ladder, a small bridge, a pole, a slide. There is a long snaking pathway. It runs away toward a hard line of blackness that he understands from Father's lessons to be a road. And past the road are houses. Real, honest to God, houses.

As he surveys his surrounds in wonder, the dull roar grows louder. Suddenly, through the trees he sees bright lights followed by a car. For a moment, he stands rooted to the spot, not thinking to protect his eyes, or hide. But then fear intrudes upon his stupor. He averts his pained gaze, collapses to the ground, spreadeagled, ready to crawl into the tunnels. But the car doesn't stop. When he glances up, he sees that it is disappearing from view, the noise fading.

He berates himself for his cowardice. He rises slowly, and in a daze follows the path to the road.

Nothing is as Father said it would be. There are houses, all still standing. They have yards, full of greenery and bright flowers.

Progeny can't reconcile the reality with the picture Father painted of the end of the world. Perhaps the remainder live on in the homes of the damned, keeping them neat. But Progeny doesn't believe this. He thinks people live here. He thinks they found another way to survive.

He should find out for sure. He should approach a house, harden his resolve, and knock on the door.

But he doesn't. Not just yet.

His attention is drawn by a strange, hairy creature, about knee high, that runs on all fours along the road toward him. It stops abruptly when it sees him, growls, turns, and disappears into one of the yards.

He hears more rumbling in the distance, more cars.

He moves farther down the road, looking from side to side, trying to decide which house looks the friendliest. But he's squinting now. His eyes have begun to sting. It occurs to him that the world is changing. It's getting brighter. He stops, peers up at the sky, and is shocked to see the colour has altered. What was black-grey is now grey-blue. And it hurts. He squeezes his eyes closed, tears beading in the corners. This isn't right.

He opens his eyes a crack, turns, and sees the first hint of a shivering orange ball of fire rising up over the horizon. He screams as it imprints itself on his retinas. He jams his eyes shut again, but still the fire burns through his lids. That light is like a blow to the head.

He buries his fists into his eye sockets, rubbing furiously. He moves blindly now, stumbling in what he hopes is back toward the entrance to the tunnels, back to darkness. But he trips, falls painfully. He skins his knees and hands on the hard surface of the road. His eyes spring open involuntarily, and he's blinded by that fire on the horizon. He screams again, clenches his eyes shut.

A door creaks open. He hears the soft pad of footsteps. And then from close behind, "Are you ok?"

He's so shocked that he swings around wildly, and his arm hits something solid, jarring. Someone grunts and curses. Pain courses through his wrist, and still the light burns. But he realises he's found a person. A real person. Because the remainder don't speak.

"I can't see," he says in a rush. "I can't see. Help me."

But the person doesn't respond.

Progeny hears more voices. He feels shadowy presences surround him, talking amongst themselves. He hears phrases like: "He might be sick," and "Don't touch him," and "The police are on their way."

The voices converge, and cover him with meaningless sounds. He no longer understands them. He's confused, and in pain, and lost in the light.

Progeny waits in a small, white room. It's been some time since his needle, but his arm still throbs. There's a burning sensation snaking out from the puncture wound, up into his shoulder, down to his wrist.

The lights are on, and even though the needle lady gave him dark goggles, his eyes hurt. They feel gritty, and water constantly.

The door to the room creaks, drawing Progeny's attention. It opens, and in walks a tall woman, greying hair, weathered face. A not unkind face.

"Hello, Progeny. My name is Doctor Gillian Reynolds. But please, call me Gillian," she says. Her voice is husky, controlled.

Progeny regards her silently. He sits stiffly on the edge of his neat, white bed. The sheets crackle when he shifts his weight.

She walks past Progeny, and eases into the single armchair in the room. She looks relaxed, as if this is her room. It's certainly not Progeny's room. It feels like a prison. From one, into the next, he thinks.

"I understand this must be very confusing for you. It's very confusing for us, so it must be confusing for you," Gillian says. She offers a hint of a sad smile.

Progeny stays silent.

Gillian crosses one leg over the other. She's holding a pen, which she begins to tap against her leg.

"We found your Father's body. I'm very sorry for your loss," she says.

"Why?" Progeny asks. He doesn't look at her, he looks past her, toward the door.

The door can't be opened from the inside. He's checked.

"I understand he mistreated you. That he kept you locked up down there. But he was still your Father."

He doesn't want to think about Father. He glances at her instead. Then he looks around the locked room. At the two-way glass. The camera in the ceiling. "When will you release me from here?"

Gillian smiles sadly. It is a knowing smile. A maternal smile.

"Five weeks at the earliest. But most likely longer than that."

"Most likely longer," Progeny repeats.

"Yes. You've never been vaccinated against the X23 virus, so you need to finish your course of injections. Your photophobia is extreme. You'll need time and treatment to help you adjust to living with sunlight. And, perhaps most importantly, we need to ensure you're mentally fit for integration. For your safety, and ours."

"So you're protecting me?" Just like Father, he thinks.

Gillian hesitates, ceases tapping her pen. "You've been away a long time, Progeny."

"Indeed."

Gillian leans forward. "We found another body in the tunnels."

Progeny tenses. The words sting as he sees his mother's desiccated corpse. "That was my mother."

Gillian doesn't say any words, but her face says more than words could. Her eyes widen, her mouth forms a little o. She covers with a cough, then eases back into the chair. She begins tapping her leg again.

In that moment, Progeny knows he's not leaving anytime soon. He doesn't understand exactly why, but he knows. These people are not the mindless remainder that Father spoke of, but they're not like him. He alarms them. And what Father did alarms them. He feels lost. Defeated.

He realises Gillian is speaking again.

"—meet once a day to discuss your upbringing and your life below ground. And your... parents," she pauses, watching Progeny. He says nothing. "At the end of each session, you'll be able to ask some questions about what has happened since you've been gone."

Progeny remembers being on his knees in the shelter, hands on his head, waiting for his question. He shakes his head.

Gillian rises lithely out of the armchair. "It's going to be okay, Progeny. This all feels strange now, I know. But I'm here to help. Engage with me fully, and we'll have you ready to face the rest of the world in no time."

He doesn't look up as Gillian leaves. He can't. Because he doesn't believe her.

The next day, Gillian enters Progeny's room brandishing a writing pad, a pencil, a sympathetic smile. Progeny lies in the bed with the crisp sheets. When he sees Gillian, he rolls away from her, stares at the wall. The sheets crackle as he moves.

"How are we today, Progeny?" Gillian asks.

He grunts, signifying nothing. His arm hurts. His eyes hurt. His chest feels tight and achy.

He hears Gillian moving. She walks around the end of his bed, and eases into the armchair. She exudes the faint scent of soap.

"I'm looking forward to finding out about you. About your life underground," she says. "But before we start, do you have any queries for me?"

Progeny doesn't say anything for a while. He's caught between wanting to snap at Gillian, and wanting to ignore her. Finally, he says, "Do you enjoy this?"

"Enjoy what, Progeny?"

"Keeping me locked up. Torturing me."

"I don't believe that is what we're doing. I'm here to assess your mental state of mind. And then to help you adjust, and to integrate into our society."

Progeny huffs, but says nothing. Gillian waits. When she realises that Progeny will say nothing further, she adds, "How we progress is up to you, Progeny. Now, tell me something about you. What do you first remember? Were you born above, or underground?"

Progeny closes his eyes. His mouth tightens into a thin line. He refuses to respond.

Gillian waits. She lets the silence build. But Progeny doesn't mind. He's lived in silence. He's comfortable there.

After what seems a long time, Gillian pushes up out of her chair, a knee clicking as she moves. Progeny hears her walk back to the door, knock. After a moment, it opens. She hesitates, then says, "Let's try again tomorrow."

Then she's gone.

Progeny ignores Gillian the next day, and the day after that. He takes joy in the tone of annoyance that creeps into her inquiries. It is a small win, he thinks. Petty, but something.

He takes further joy in her absence the following day. And the day after that.

But his joy doesn't last. Left by himself, he realises that with Gillian's company, or without, he's still stuck in this room. At least underground, he had space to move, to fish, to dig. But in here, all he has is questions, and needles, and lights that sting.

There's something dark forming inside him. Something cavernous. He's worrying at it, giving it form. A tunnel of his own making.

"What do you remember of your mother?" Gillian asks. She sits in the armchair again, watching Progeny watch her. He's hunched over, perched on the end of the bed. It's late evening. His dinner remains untouched on a tray on the bedside table. The once earthy scent of the soup is morphing into something rancid as it cools.

Progeny stares blankly for a long time through his dark goggles. He shifts his gaze beyond Gillian, to focus on a stain on the wall. He licks his lips. Reluctantly, he speaks. Slowly. Petulantly. "I remember her corpse. Her bones. She smelt like dust."

Gillian nods, her pencil makes scratching noises as she moves it across her writing pad. "What about before she died?"

Progeny snorts a mirthless laugh. "Nothing."

"I see. What about your father then? What was he like?"

Progeny flinches. He feels the sting of the switch under his arm. He hears Father's yells. He watches him disappear under the collapse of the tunnel.

"He was like you."

"Me?"

"You and your kind. He also locked me up and told me it was for my benefit."

Gillian frowns. "What else did he do? What did you talk about with him? What did he teach you?"

He sneers, opens his mouth to answer. But then he sees Gillian watching him, waiting, her pen poised above the pad. And he suddenly imagines her sitting in that chair for many years to come. Repeating this performance. Day after day. His bravado falters. Tears well, his lips quiver. He feels like he is falling.

"Please," he croaks, "Let me go. I won't tell anyone. Please. I can't cope in here anymore."

Gillian sighs, cocks her head. Progeny thinks she intends to look sympathetic. She looks condescending. "I'm sorry. I am, but—"

"Let me go, god damnit," Progeny yells suddenly, jumping down from the bed, fists clenched with impotent rage.

At first, Gillian's face shows shock. But then it becomes something else. A cold expression. A hard expression.

She rises from the armchair, turns and carefully places her pencil and pad on the seat of the chair. She moves to the door, knocks, and after a moment it opens. At first, Progeny thinks she is leaving him. But then she holds the door ajar, looks back at Progeny, and says, "Come with me."

His eyes widen. But his legs quickly move.

Progeny follows Gillian out into a sterile, white corridor. The sound of her shoes on the linoleum seems loud to Progeny. He licks his lips, and watches her walk away. The corridor is dimly lit. It smells of disinfectant. He waits for the men to grab him, to shove him back into his room. He waits, but they don't appear. And so he hurries after Gillian.

At the end of the hall is an elevator. Gillian swipes a key card, waits.

"Where are we going?" Progeny asks, his fury left back in his room. He's certain she's not releasing him, and yet he hopes.

"Up," Gillian says.

The elevator doors open with a ding, and Gillian steps inside. Progeny follows. The scent is human, stale. What is this? he wonders.

A short ride, and the doors open. Gillian steps out of the lift and makes a hard right. When Progeny follows, he finds her already climbing a metal staircase, her footfall clanging.

Gillian waits for him at the top, in front of a door. When he catches up to her, she says, "Are you ready?"

But she doesn't allow him time to respond. She wrenches the door open and Progeny is assaulted by light. Not the sun, it's not that bright, but it still hurts, even with the goggles. He clamps his eyes shut, turns his head away, but Gillian grabs him by the wrist and, with gentle force, guides him through the door.

He instantly notices eddies of air around him, and knows he is outside. The air smells acrid and oily, not like before. And then there is the soundtrack. A strange, loud chorus of roaring, and honking.

"Look," she demands. "This is what you wanted, so look."

Slowly, hesitantly, he allows his eyes to open a crack. The artificial light comes from monolithic structures that reach up into the sky like the roots of an upside down tree. They're mostly glass. And they glow with checkerboard patterns of light and dark.

When his eyes follow the tallest tower up to its highest point, he sees the black of the night sky beyond. But there is barely a star to be seen here. When he looks back down below, he sees strips of neon. And in between, parallel lines of white lights, and red, moving slowly like two giant eels swimming in opposite directions. That is where the honking and roars come from. It's all unpleasant.

Overwhelming. He doesn't know where to look. Or how to block out the noise.

Gillian releases his arm. His legs wobble, but he keeps his balance. He turns his back on the city. Thankfully, looking the other way, he finds less light. And what lights there are, are diffused, mainly located at ground level, but spreading outward for miles, and miles.

"This is the world, Progeny," Gillian says, drawing his attention. "You really think you're ready for this?"

"I... I..."

"If we let you go, where would you go?" she asks. She's speaking with a firm tone, enunciating each word. He opens his mouth, closes it. He glances back uncertainly at the city. It retains its chaotic splendour.

"Do you have family? Or friends here? We haven't found any, but perhaps you know better?"

He swallows, shakes his head. "I don't know."

"Where would you live?"

"I... I don't know."

"People need to work to survive in the city. If you work, you make money so you can pay for a home, and food. Did your father explain this to you?"

Progeny nods.

"Then what would you do? What skills do you have?"

He shakes his head again. He feels tears stabbing at his eyes. He blinks hard to hold them back. "I can dig," he offers quietly.

She exhales for a long time, like all of the air in her lungs is tainted and she wants to be done with it. "Progeny, you are a ward of the State. We are responsible for you both here and out there. I don't gain from keeping you here forever. But I would be failing my duty if I released you to become homeless and to starve. My job is to prepare you for life outside. But this," she says, with a sweeping arm gesture toward the city, "is beyond you right now. Jesus," she hisses, "let me help. That's what I'm trying to do. I'm not your father."

All Progeny can think about are stars, or the lack of them. He glances up again and wonders where they have gone. He remembers the millions of pinpricks of light he saw when he first rose from the tunnels. A promise of something infinite. It's there, he thinks. It must be. Out there. Somewhere. He regards Gillian again, and finds that her expression has softened.

"How we go from here is up to you, Progeny. You can ignore me, demand to be released before you are ready, and stay with us. Perhaps forever. Or, you can accept that this will take time, and then get to work."

Progeny takes a breath, and takes one last lingering look up at the darkness. When he looks back at Gillian, he nods.

Back in his room, locked up again, Progeny lies awake. He stares at the ceiling, but his mind is a long way away.

He's in his dark place. The tunnel he's built inside. Around him fly Gillian's words, along with his father's, and his own defeated thoughts. But, for all of that, he doesn't feel quite so alone down here. He may not see a way out, not right now anyway, but he knows there is a starlit sky waiting for him up above somewhere. He's proved that to himself once before, not very long ago.

Which is why he's decided to change course. He's decided to start digging up.

*See Michael Gardner's story "All That Remains"
online at Metaphorosis.
If you liked it, leave a comment. Authors love
that!
Remember to subscribe to our e-mail updates so
you'll know when new stories are posted.*

About the story

Despite current events, this story wasn't inspired by the coronavirus. I wrote this a good six months before COVID-19 broke out.

I'd been reading a number of dystopian fantasy and horror stories at the time. I began wondering what might happen to a doomsday prepper who hid away from the end of the world, only to find out years later that the world hadn't ended after all. And then, what if that person brought a child with them.

I found that tension interesting, so started to play with it, and along came Progeny. A man-child, really, with a lot to learn about the shortcomings of his father, and himself.

A question for the author

Q: Can beautiful things be funny?

A: I think funny moments can be beautiful, so beautiful things must be funny.

As an example, I was trying not to laugh at my daughter the other day who was doing her best to avoid going to bed. I failed in my attempt to be stern, and ended up laughing at her antics, which made her laugh in return. I was wondering where she got her cheeky sense of humour. And in that moment, I realised she was growing up in front of me, becoming her own, unique person. I couldn't help but think that sharing such a moment in her life was beautiful. As well as being funny.

About the author

Michael Gardner is an economist by day, a writer of fantasy and horror by night. He lives in Canberra, Australia, with his patient wife and two wonderful kids. The experience of fatherhood continues to find its way into his stories. His work has appeared in *Writers of the Future Volume 36, Aurealis*, and of course, *Metaphorosis*. He is also a two-time finalist for the Aurealis Awards. You can find out more about Michael and his work at www.michael-s-gardner.com.

Joy (Unplugged)

B.C. van Tol

A reddish moon clung to the horizon like a faded blood stain that wouldn't wash out. Joy shivered, looking at the moon's human-like face from her attic window, wishing she could pull him to her. Together, they could agonize in this lonely house atop the hill. From afar, his mouth hung agape, as though wailing in silent operatic sorrow. The silence pervaded the dark, motionless town nestled in the valley below. From Joy's vantage point, the town seemed nothing more than a crumbling diorama of miniature homes and shops. After being alone for over a year, Joy wondered whether she'd ever see anyone again.

She switched on her electric candle and placed it on the windowsill in the attic. The soft yellow glow served as her beacon to those who might Detach in the night, stumbling confused and withered into a reality they'd long since abandoned.

When her eyes grew weary, she climbed into bed beside a row of pillows arranged to look like another person already asleep under the covers. She slid her arm around a pillow, tracing the scars in its casing where she'd sewn its many rips and tears. It wouldn't survive much longer, she knew. And if the solitude continued, neither would she.

"Goodnight," she whispered, clinging desperately to the pillow. As if in response, the centuries-old house creaked eerily from a passing breeze. Some sound was always better than none.

Nobody came that night.

Joy arose at dawn, kissed the top of her pretend pillow person, and retrieved the candle from the attic. It was a clear day, and she could see the town's distant clock tower. Its hands had given up at 8:34 one April morning before her twenty-third birthday. That had been over a decade ago.

Beyond the town, standing like sentries in an enemy army, were the giant wind turbines that generated the energy supply for the town's Virtual Lifestyle Attachments (un-affectionately known to Joy as ViLiAs). A network transmitter column glowered like an emperor in the center of the turbine field. The column was responsible for luring the townspeople into a completely customizable, full-sensory trance. The sun glinted off its steel armor. A red light blinked at the top, taunting her the way the moon did.

Because Joy was the sole person not participating in ViLiAs and had no wind turbines of her own, she pedaled on her stationary bicycle, which charged the battery in her electric candle. The house, devoid of all other electricity, had once belonged to her grandmother. When the ViLiAs claimed Joy's mother as one of their earliest victims, Gran had stripped the house of its appliances and wiring, even going so far as to plaster over the old electric sockets.

Gran once said, "Humans got along just fine for thousands of years without electricity."

But humans always had each other, Joy thought as she pedaled. Not for the first time, she considered whether it was worse to live a fake life with real people than a real life with a fake pillow person.

At least Gran had kept a wind-up record player and a hodge-podge collection of vinyls. Joy let Chopin soothe her loneliness as she tended the garden for the rest of the morning.

In the afternoon, Joy baked a loaf of bread in the wood-burning stone hearth built into the house's original foundation. She kept her windows open so the scent of baking would drift outside. Someone out there might long for fresh food.

That evening, she practiced on Gran's upright piano. She'd left the front door open so as to fill the hillside with music. The sun had begun to set, and she could hardly see the black and white keys in front of her.

During rests in the music, she heard footsteps stumbling onto the porch. When she turned around, a man loomed in the doorway. His clothes hung like rags, and his head seemed loosely attached to his gaunt frame.

She rose, her movements slow though her heart raced. The Detached were like skittish, starving animals. His eyes scanned the living room while she leaned awkwardly against the piano. "I've food," she offered, hoping she didn't sound as desperate as she felt.

When he took a tentative step forward, she ventured into the kitchen and put a plate of bread and jam on the table, eagerly listening toward the door. Then came the sound of his feet shuffling across the wooden floors.

When he took a seat, she resisted the urge to sit beside him, to not-so-accidentally brush his hand as he reached for the jam. Patience is a curse, she thought, as he ran his fingers over the bread, getting jam on his fingertips, as if not quite sure it was real. He would have been accustomed to neuro-simulated taste, since the ViLiAs fed people bland, liquified nutrients through a feeding tube. Of the food sludge, there was endless supply, since everything was recycled through biowaste tubes and re-processed in underground factories overseen by robotic machinery. Joy shuddered.

Fastidiously, he ate, inspecting every morsel, even the crumbs on the plate. After the bread was gone, the man sat for a long time with his eyes closed. Joy knew better than to disturb him. Most Detached persons took a while to distinguish reality from what they had conjured and customized as part of their Virtual Lifestyle package. She gazed through the kitchen window at the last sliver of sun descending from view and listened as the birds outside quieted into their nests.

When he looked up again, she said, "I have a spare room upstairs. You're welcome to stay." She left out the word 'forever'.

A curious-minded Detached person might stay a week until the Withdrawal became unbearable. With fortitude, they might survive Withdrawal and stay a month before something else called to them—a sense of adventure, a sense of fear, a sense of loss. Eventually, they all left.

The man seemed to consider her offer. He had probably forgotten what it meant to feel tired. Or feel anything at all, for that matter. He opened his mouth to speak, but only air came out.

"Your voice will return with time. Come, you could do with some rest."

Though he stood a foot taller and would have been formidable had he not wasted away, Joy had no fear of being raped. According to Gran, ViLiAs made men impotent. Sometimes permanently. It didn't matter, however. Once Attached, anyone could experience every pleasure in a virtual setting. Even have virtual children.

They ascended the stairs by the light of Joy's electric candle, their bodies casting long shadows on the wall. When an animal screeched somewhere in the night, he jumped, grabbing onto the railing.

"Just an owl," she said and then showed him to his room. Before shutting the door, she added, "It helps to listen to the sound of your breath. It's a reminder that you're still alive."

Without the usual sense of gloom, Joy climbed to the attic and placed the electric candle in the window.

The next morning as she tended her garden, she glanced up at his window and saw him gazing at the woods behind the house. His expression resembled that of a lost child. Her heart felt an invisible bond extending to him, as if she'd reached out her hand and he'd taken it.

Oh, to feel the touch of a hand! she thought. The last human contact she'd had was a brushing of arms one year, five months, and three days ago. Joy kept a written log of such things. The other arm belonged to a Detached woman who had stayed with Joy for four days and then mysteriously left in the night. Joy blamed the woman's departure on the physical contact. The Detached seemed unable to endure it in the first days after returning to reality.

This day, the clouds were plentiful, and she could smell rain in the air. Just as she finished picking green beans, the first drops fell. Inside, Joy found the man standing at her fireplace mantle, entranced by a photograph. She said, "That's my grandmother. She raised me. In this house, in fact."

He turned and studied Joy, not realizing or maybe not caring that to inspect another human being was once considered rude. She took the opportunity to study him as well. He had somber deep brown eyes, but also sallow skin and plump lips hidden beneath a scraggly, brittle beard. Matted dark hair dangled from his head. He scratched at it with bony hands.

"I'm Joy," she whispered.

His voice was barely a rasp. "I'm... MightyAugust8501." He frowned, something not quite right. "I mean August. Just August."

She guessed he'd not used this name for many years.

He pointed to Gran in the photograph, his eyebrows raised as if to ask where Gran was.

Joy said, "If you look out the window, beyond those trees is a clearing where sunbeams fall through the branches. Gran used to say that the sunbeams looked like the silk of her wedding dress." Joy sighed. "Have you ever felt real silk, August?"

He shook his head.

"I buried her in the wedding dress in that clearing. Carried her in my arms all the way. After the sickness, she weighed so little..." Joy's thoughts trailed off. She knew she must be careful. Sorrow was a dangerous companion for someone so often alone. "Anyway, that was eight years ago." Eight years, one month, and twenty-two days. Nine Detached visitors in all that time.

Later, August sat on the couch, while she played the piano. At first, he covered his ears against the sound. Joy took no offense. When he lowered his hands and began to sway his head from side to side, she smiled because it meant his soul hadn't died.

"You're welcome to stay as long as you wish," she said.

That night, after August retired to his room, Joy climbed into her own bed next to the pillow person. For a moment, she put her arm around it. It smelled faintly of mildew and felt rough against her skin. Joy shoved the pillow person onto the floor where she stomped on it until its scars opened and it bled stuffing.

"Never again," she said.

When she awoke the next morning, she found August again in front of her fireplace mantle, admiring a different photo. Tears streaked his cheeks.

"Is something wrong?" She curtailed the urge to hug him, to wipe away his tears and stroke his matted hair.

"Do you have children?" he asked.

"No, that's me. I'm four years old, sitting on Gran's lap at the park. Back when the park wasn't a wind turbine field. It's the last picture ever taken of me."

Over breakfast of bread and jam, he asked, "Why do you do all this for a stranger?"

"Don't worry. You don't owe me anything."

"Why?" he said more forcefully. Charity was not a trait of an addicted society. Kindness would have been to him like a strange dream.

"It's what I do," she said.

He crossed his arms, unsatisfied.

"It's a long story."

"Good," he said.

With a sigh, she settled into a chair opposite him. "When I was little, people finally began to realize how addictive ViLiAs were, and some addicts decided to Detach on their own. Gran and I took in several of these people over the years. Nobody else was around to help. We showed the Detached how to return to a natural life. Or at least, we tried."

In truth, Joy and her gran had helped nearly three dozen Detached work through their Withdrawal. Of those, four had died in the process. Those who survived eventually left with their newfound lives or invented some excuse to go back to the Attachment. "Now Gran is buried in the clearing, where the silken sunshine comes in. I continue our work all by myself." Joy shrugged. "It's the only life I know."

"Will you take me?" he asked.

"To the clearing?"

"I want to see the silk."

Later, they walked through the woods, crossed the stream in their bare feet, and climbed the hill to the clearing. August's face filled with wonder as he cupped one of the silken sunbeams falling through the branches above. Then he did something he hadn't done yet: he laughed, a shuddering breathy sound that made Joy think of new life coming into the world.

"I didn't think the sun could feel soft," he said, amazed.

Joy laughed, too, despite herself. A patch of light covered his head, and she could see color returning to his cheeks. Good, she thought. He'll need to be healthy for what comes next.

After dinner, Joy put on some records. She began with the classical, spritely Mozart. Food for the soul and the making of a good temperament, Gran always said. August bobbed his head to the music.

The next morning, she gasped when she saw him. He'd trimmed back his beard and had given himself a haircut. Joy could hardly recognize him, but despite the unevenness of his trimming, he less resembled a feral animal and more a person.

"I found a pair of scissors in the bathroom," he said. "I couldn't take the itching anymore. Before, when I was Attached, I remember scratching, vaguely, like it was someone else's itch. Eventually, I scratched so much I must have knocked off my electrodes, because I woke up gagging on my feeding tube."

"It must have been terrifying." Joy outstretched her hand to give his shoulder a comforting squeeze. He tensed at her approach, and she whirled around, ashamed.

Breaking the tension, he pointed to a bowl on the kitchen table. "I picked you some strawberries. I wanted to do more. For you."

Then never leave me, she would have replied.

He tapped some keys on her piano. "Is it hard to learn?" he asked, pressing a shrill-toned cluster of notes in the highest register. He winced and withdrew his hand from the keys.

"Yes, but if you enjoy playing, you don't notice it's difficult."

"Like the Attachment," he whispered.

Joy played a happy tune from memory. She had forgotten its name, but it reminded her of the stream's delicate surface and how it caught the sun's reflection, making it dance. When the song ended, she saw through the living room window the waxing moon hanging romantically in a clear sky full of bright stars.

"I can't hear the moon's terrible singing when you're here," she said. "He looks almost peaceful now. Like a child yawning before sleep."

August appeared wistful for a moment. "When I first Detached, I was so disoriented that the moon frightened me. I wandered in the woods for I don't know how long, trying to hide from him under the trees, but he was always watching. Then I heard your piano, and I saw the light in your window. These did not frighten me, so I came here to you."

Instinctively, Joy grasped his hand. The touch sent reverberations up her arm and down her back. August cried out and yanked his hand away.

"No! I'm sorry!" she said, horrified at what she had done.

August clutched his hand to his chest protectively, his eyes darting to the front door.

Please stay! she wanted to shout, but the situation required calmness. Softly, slowly, she said, "You probably haven't experienced human touch in many years. Touching another person isn't the same as using your fingers to eat or feeling the sun on your face. When you've been deprived of it for so long, a first touch can hurt. It hurt me as well."

"I should do more for you..." he said, slowly extending his hand back out to her, cringing and wrinkling his nose like touch were a bad smell. The temptation to take it again was almost more than she could bear.

She shook her head. "It's okay."

He dropped his hand, clearly relieved. "Perhaps tomorrow," he said.

"Perhaps."

When she woke the next morning, she could not find August anywhere in the house. At first, the seeds of panic grew, and she worried her transgression had caused him to flee in the night. That is, until she found him outside crouched over the stream, his hair glistening with water. His cheeks had more health than she had yet seen, and he smelled fresher.

"A bath?" she asked.

He nodded. "I can't sit still today. I could hardly sleep last night."

He did not offer her his hand again this morning. She would not remind him. Not now, at the first signs of Withdrawal: restlessness, sleeplessness. By tomorrow, he would have the headaches. The day after, the sweats, the body aches. And the next day, fever, shakes, or even ... she didn't dare think it.

She set him to pulling weeds in the garden while she picked some lettuces. He pulled a few and began to stare out into the direction of town. She followed his gaze to the network transmitter column, which occasionally winked at them with its red come-hither beacon at the top. If only she could snuff it out.

"My gran always said to look in the direction you are headed."

August hastily pulled some more weeds. "Have you ever tried ViLiAs?"

"No," she said. She feared such discussion would only keep his mind on the subject.

"Oh." His gaze returned to the network transmitter column.

Jealous of the column's continued hold on August, she said, "I do know what it means to feel unbearably restless." Once more, she had his attention. She wiped some sweat from her brow with her sleeve and continued working as she spoke. "In my late teenage years, I had boundless energy and found I couldn't sit still. I argued with Gran constantly, something I'm ashamed of now, but at the time, I had no idea what had gotten into me. Gran patiently let me rant or put me to labor-intensive chores to burn my energy off.

"One day, as I stood in this very garden, I heard the clock tower chiming. I felt the pull of the world beckoning me to explore it. That day, I said to Gran, 'I need to leave and make my own way.' I thought she would put up a fuss or forbid me. Instead, she kissed my forehead and sent me off with a loaf of bread and a flask of water." Joy still remembered Gran's warm, firm kiss on her forehead.

"Where did you go?" August asked, leaning forward.

"First, I went into the hills, but then the hills turned into bald-faced mountains. I was not so foolish as to think I could cross them alone, so I turned and wandered the forest for a time, living mostly off berries. I realized very quickly that with freedom came loneliness. I became homesick and wanted nothing more than to hug my gran."

"Did you go home?"

"No. I was stubborn. Instead, I went into the town."

"What did you find?"

"More loneliness. Not a soul walked the streets. No children played outside. Most windows were boarded up completely. Eventually, I came to a cottage on a street lined with fallen trees. I imagined it was once charming, but the grasses had grown so high that the cottage appeared short and stubby, like a dollhouse for a child. It had one window that was not boarded, and I peeked in. A person lay on the floor of the front room—a woman so emaciated I could not have guessed at her age. She would have looked dead, if not for one trembling, outstretched arm reaching for something not quite within grasp. You see, despite having tumbled from her couch, she was still Attached. Her ViLiAs face mask was still in place, and sensory electrodes dotted her body. Then I noticed what she reached for—her feeding tube, which had evidently fallen out some time earlier.

"I just couldn't understand it. Was her addiction so strong that she would starve to death, inches from nourishment because she couldn't Detach for mere seconds to save her own life?

"I banged on the window. 'Take off the mask!' I shouted. If she heard me, she showed no sign of it. Had I known better— or perhaps, had I not been so lonely—I would've left her there. Instead, I broke the window, and I climbed in. Then I made the mistake of Detaching her."

August grimaced, evidently remembering the shock of his own Detachment.

"The woman screamed so loudly that it echoed through the valley. I expected the police to come or neighbors to check on her."

August shook his head. "I don't suppose anyone did."

"No," she replied somberly. "It gets worse. I grabbed the woman by the shoulder. 'You need to eat!' I told her. The jolt of Detachment and the sudden human contact made her berserk. As I tried to calm her, she clawed at me with nails that hadn't been clipped in a long time. Then she bit my arm." Joy rolled up her sleeve and showed August the shiny depressed scar where the woman had taken a healthy chunk of flesh. "When she bit me, I dropped her on the floor. There was a horrible thud, and then she was still. I thought I killed her. I panicked, bleeding. I put the Attachments back on her and re-inserted her feeding tube, in hopes it would coax her to stay alive. Or at least relieve the suffering I'd caused in trying to help."

"Did she die?"

Joy shrugged. "I sat next to her the whole day, just watching her breathing to make sure it didn't stop. Hours later, when it started to get dark, I put my hand on her chest to make sure I could feel it rise and fall. I sang to her to drown out the moon that stared, judging me, through the broken window.

"By nightfall, the bite in my arm had become swollen and infected. I held it up to the moonlight and saw two red lines under my skin creeping up to my shoulder. If I stayed with her much longer, I knew I'd die of sepsis, so I left her there on the floor. I went out into the night, looking for Gran's candle in the attic up at the top of the hill. I stumbled for hours, following that little flicker of hope, fever shaking me and pus weeping down my forearm. I followed the candle, ashamed of myself, terrified Gran would never forgive me."

"Did she forgive?"

Joy shut her eyes, remembering. When she'd reached the house, the clock tower had struck midnight. She saw Gran's silhouette standing out on the porch.

"She asked me, 'Joy, have you learned anything in your travels?' I knelt down before her, half in fatigue, half in penance, and I said, 'I've learned more than I care to.' Gran helped me to my feet, embraced me. 'I can hear it in your voice. Come inside now. You're home.'" Joy could still feel her gran's arms around her, and her eyes misted over.

August gazed back toward the network transmitter column once more, a different air about him, as though seeing his past clearly for the first time, seeing the terrible fall of humanity from which he'd dragged himself.

"Home," he said, slipping his hand in hers.

Joy felt as if she'd won her first true battle against the network transmitter column, still blinking at her with red scorn.

The next day, Joy awoke to find August pacing downstairs.

"I can't sit still. Every time I stop moving, I think my bones will crawl out of my skin. What's happening to me?"

She examined his eyes. They were bloodshot and had dark circles beneath them. His breath was snappy. "It's the early stages of Withdrawal."

He resumed pacing. "I keep thinking I'll die unless I re-Attach myself. Like there are invisible cords wrapped around my arms, pulling me back to it..." His speech became so rapid that she could no longer understand him.

"You must eat. Your body needs the fuel."

After he wolfed down some bread, she put a feather duster in his jittery hands.

"You see the fireplace mantle? Start dusting there. When you're done, do the bookcases. After that, the cabinets. If you can't keep still, keep yourself busy."

"I'm scared," he said, taking her hand.

"It's normal," she assured him. It was the best she could promise. There was still a chance he could die.

While he dusted, she began to prepare enough food to last several days. When he finished dusting, he asked her what to do next. So, she handed him an axe. "My wood pile is getting low," she said, pointing to a fallen tree. "If you get dizzy or breathless, stop."

Though he didn't appear strong, the Withdrawal restlessness evidently gave him enough energy to wield the axe. Grunting with each swing, he chopped the wood until he stumbled away from the tree in exhaustion. By that time, most of the afternoon had passed.

Joy helped him back into the house and up to his room. "Something's wrong," he said, his voice unsteady. "My heart keeps skipping, and I feel a shadow creeping toward me."

"Do you still feel like your bones will crawl out of your skin?"

He blinked down at her from his tired eyes. "No."

"See? You're doing a fine job. Now just rest."

His breath came in rapid, shallow waves while she watched over him from a chair beside his bed. Eventually, he slept.

Joy did not put the candle in the attic window that night. She kept it at August's bedside, along with a basket of bread and a pail of fresh water. He awoke in the night writhing and sweating. She put a cool compress on his forehead. He vomited, and she cleaned him. Sometimes he spoke in desperate tones. "Let me go back. Just for a few minutes..."

"You're too sick to go anywhere just now. When you're better, you can go wherever you want," she said.

"Everything hurts. My eyes hurt. My teeth hurt. The air around my body hurts!"

"You're purging addiction from your system."

She dripped some water onto his lips, and he licked it off, eventually drifting back to sleep. The next day, he spent hours curled in a ball lying on his side, moaning, shivering with fever.

"I'm dying," he said. He grabbed the sleeve of her shirt, ripping the seam at her shoulder. "Am I dying?" She could not deny it. "I need to go back. Please... Let me go."

He tried to get up from the bed but discovered his legs could not carry him. He fell to the floor and screamed in pain. As she rushed to help him back into the bed, he began to thrash wildly, and she worried he'd bite her.

"You tricked me! You made me swing the axe so many times that it sucked the life from me. You did it on purpose to keep me here!"

She knew it was the Withdrawal speaking, not her August, but it hurt all the same. Gran had always warned her not to get too close to the Detached—to become Attached to them. "They will pull you down with them," she had said. "You can do your best to help, and at the end of the day, if you manage to save one, that will fulfill you more than anything." However, Gran had always had Joy. What did Gran know of utter desolation and the wretched, humiliating need to cling to another living soul?

"It's not fair," she whispered once August had fallen asleep again. Joy ran her fingers over his cheeks.

When August woke next, he could hardly move. His lips had cracked, and the whites of his eyes had turned blood red from burst capillaries. He had fever rashes on his neck and chest. "Joy?" he said with a scratchy voice.

"I'm here."

"It doesn't hurt anymore. Will you tell me a story?" he asked, his eyes drooping. "Please."

Her arms ached from the days and nights tending to him. Her head throbbed from lack of sleep, and her back had grown sore from sitting in a wooden armchair while he slept. In their moments of shared pain, Joy had felt more connected to August than ever. Her August.

"Tell me about your parents," he said.

"It's not a happy story."

"Please." He held out his hand, and she wrapped her fingers around his.

"I don't know who my father is. Gran told me that someone took advantage of my mother after she became Attached. I was the result. My mother carried me to term, delivered me, all without Detaching once. The doctors said she'd miscarry if she went into Withdrawal. I was born healthy enough, but the birth coupled with addiction took a toll on her body. Gran, for the one and only time, hooked herself up to the ViLiAs to ask my mother what name to give me. My mother named me Joy. That's all I have of her. She died two days later."

As August's eyes filled with sorrow, Joy regretted telling him such a mournful tale. In a happier tone, she continued. "Gran said that my mother adored Beethoven's 'Ode to Joy,' and that's where my name came from. When I was a girl, I used to make Gran play the record over and over."

"I would love to hear it."

Joy set up the record player on the floor by his bed, put "Ode to Joy" into the spinner, and let it flood into the room like a pink and yellow sunrise dancing over snowcapped mountains.

At the end, he said, "This music is everything that is life. It doesn't lie or give false impressions."

Joy nodded, realizing for the first time that the song—and therefore her name— was as much a warning as it was a gift. Her mother had wanted Joy to live. To not follow in her footsteps.

Then he cried, "Look what I've done to myself! I don't know how I could have ever chosen a Virtual Lifestyle over this one. Or how..." his voice trailed off.

She wanted him to say, "Or how I could ever go back," but he didn't. Even now, she could sense something still tying him to his old life.

Give it time, she thought. If he survived this night, he would certainly pull through. Moreover, if he pulled through, he'd probably stay several more weeks. Then maybe, just maybe, he would be the one to stay forever, and together, they could continue the mission of saving the Detached.

August fell asleep once more, looking ashen as the moon. She did not take her eyes off his rising and falling chest. Sometimes his breathing became so shallow that she put her hand to his mouth to make sure she felt the exchange of air. Then he simply stopped breathing altogether.

At first, she thought it was a trick of her eyes. After all, she had been awake for days. She jammed her finger into his neck and felt a weak, uneven pulse. Screaming his name, she shook him, hoping he'd wake up. When that failed, she pumped his chest with her hands as Gran had taught her to do. She poured her own breath into his lungs, wishing it would pass some of her life into him. She did this until he coughed and sputtered.

Heaving, sweaty, and tear-streaked, she sank back into the chair, fully drained of the last energy in her reserves. She resumed her pulse and breath vigil, fighting the urgency of sleep with the fear that if she gave in to her sagging eyelids, she might awake to find him dead. She prayed there would be no need to resuscitate him a second time, for she simply did not have the strength.

Eventually, sleep claimed her as she slumped in the chair, her neck craning to one side. When she opened her eyes, the sun shone on August's slack face. She leapt up, fearing the worst, then she saw his chest rise. She saw it rise again and then a third time. They were full, restorative breaths. A finger to his pulse confirmed his heartbeat had returned to a normal pace. She took his hand, and sleep consumed her again.

This time, when she woke, it was still daylight. Or had she slept so long that it was daylight again? August was no longer in his bed, and a blanket had been draped around her shoulders. She got up from the chair, her knees sore and wobbling.

"August?" she called down from the top of the stairs. He did not respond. Hanging onto the railing to support her cramped legs, she descended to her living room.

"August?" Again, no response, and she despaired. Could he, after all they'd just endured, have returned to his Attachment? Surely, it would kill her.

Joy flung open the front door and nearly knocked August off the porch.

"Oh, you're awake," he said. He had tucked a single wildflower into the pocket of his shirt.

"I thought you left." She smoothed her hair, relieved she had been wrong and feeling guilty for having doubted him.

"No," he replied with an air of hesitation. She sensed an invisible "not yet" strung to the end of his thoughts. He looked out into the brightness of the day and faced the town. Drifting clouds cast blobs of shadows over the clock tower, the wind turbines, and the relentlessly blinking network transmitter column.

"How do you feel?"

His eyes still focused in the direction of town, he sighed wistfully. "Like I've just been born."

"Come inside, let's eat. We both could use the nourishment."

They shared a meal in silence. When it was over, he turned to her. "I'm sorry for how I behaved. For the things I said. The things I did. I'm ashamed."

She flitted her hand. "It's nothing. I've seen it before."

He knelt before her on the floor, taking the flower from his shirt pocket and holding it up to her. The delicate purple petals had already begun to wilt.

Joy swallowed hard, sensing the approach of bad news. "Shall we listen to some more records today?" She did not take the flower.

"I've been alone my entire life. Physically alone, but I never noticed it. Emotionally, mentally, I've had the entire world full of people just a brain wave away."

"All digital tricks and lies."

"Yes. But it was all I knew for many years." Their eyes met, and he touched her hair, tucking the flower behind her ear.

She didn't want to hear any more. As she pulled away from him, he grabbed her shoulder.

Joy squeezed her eyes shut. "Don't."

"I have to leave here, Joy. My wife…"

She felt her throat constrict.

"…my wife is back there. I know our marriage was virtual. The life we built, the home we made … all fabricated."

Joy shook her head violently.

August sobbed. "Even our children…"

She could take no more, and wrested herself free. She ran to the living room and wilted into the couch.

He followed her. "My own children are not even real! Can you believe that? In the ViLiAs, it seemed normal. But out here, my soul is sick from having spent years of my life caring for people … things … that don't exist. These beings created in my image, with my eyes and my chin." His voice broke.

He went to the photographs on the mantle and picked up the one of Joy and Gran at the park. "I'll never have pictures with my children. I'll never truly be able to hold them in my hands." He held his hands out to her. "Joy, I've never even looked upon my wife with my own eyes. Never caressed her cheek or kissed her lips. Never touched her hair the way I've touched yours. I don't even know if she looks the same as her avatar in the system. I modeled my avatar after the real me, but that's not a requirement. She lives here in our town, but we've never met."

"So you'll go back to her—to the Attachment—after all this. Fine, then."

"I'll beg my wife to Detach. Convince her to join your cause—our cause. Will you help me?"

Joy crossed her arms and turned away. "I've always said you're free to go. Everyone leaves."

He took the photograph of her and Gran and pressed it into her hands. "You don't understand. This picture has inspired me. I'm disgusted by how much I've missed of life, including the chance to have real children. Not perfect digital representations of them. I want to clean up messes and argue over stupid things and teach them about life. You can't teach a computerized child—it already knows everything."

Joy shook her head. "But you won't be able to have real children. Not without a fertility doctor."

"After I bring my wife back, we can rescue doctors, neighbors, friends. Let's save our town, Joy. You and I can do it. We'll continue what your gran started."

She rolled up her sleeve and pointed at the scar from when the Detached woman bit her arm. "It doesn't work that way," she said through clenched teeth.

"I have to try. I just…" he ran his hand through his hair. "I can't not try."

"You're free to go."

"I promise you, Joy." He cupped her face in his hands, and for a moment, she thought he loved her. "I promise you," he said, emphasizing every syllable. "I will come back."

"Take some bread with you," she said. "And a flask of water."

August nodded, and then he left. When he shut the door, she ran to the window to watch him walk into the folds of the town below in the valley. "He'll never come back," she whispered. When she turned around, it was there—all the silence and loneliness that had been hiding since the day he showed up.

Joy gritted her teeth and got on her stationary bicycle. "No sense in milling about." After, she boiled his bedsheets and hung them to dry on the line. The breeze and the sun would infuse them with crispness and remove his scent. She'd simply start over, just as she'd always done. She washed her hair and let that, too, dry in the remaining sunlight before the sky turned pink and orange.

When night was certain, she took the sheets from the line, folded them, and put them away. She cut herself a slice of bread, and though she had no appetite, she forced herself to eat it, one nibble at a time. Joy tried, and failed, with each breath to push the memory of August's face from her mind. Not just his face, but all the hopes she had pinned on him.

Finally, she took the candle and climbed the stairs to put it in the attic window. August is down there somewhere, she thought. Down there with the rest of the world while I remain alone forever.

In her room, she found the pillow person still wounded on the floor where she'd left it. Her bed was empty. Her house was empty. Her heart was empty.

Instead of searching for sleep, Joy climbed into the attic. Then she shoved the candle out the window. The little orange glow fell like an ember until the glass crunched against the ground, snuffing out the light.

In the darkness, in her nightgown, she found the axe. She threw it over her shoulder and followed the blinking light of the network transmitter column. The lure of her enemy beckoning to her. Daring her to make her last stand. Alone, as always.

Above her, the moon gaped with silent laughter.

See B.C. van Tol's story "Joy (Unplugged)" online at Metaphorosis.
If you liked it, leave a comment. Authors love that!
Remember to subscribe to our e-mail updates so you'll know when new stories are posted.

About the story

"Joy (Unplugged)" is a product of multiple inspirations. The first is my great grandmother, who, despite not having much, would leave food out on her porch for impoverished people traveling through town looking for jobs during the Great Depression. The second is a curiosity about potential psychological and societal impacts of immersive technology. The third inspiration comes from interviews I've both read and conducted related to forms of technology addiction. I enjoy taking disparate ideas and weaving them together to create a story.

A question for the author

Q: What kind of non-fiction do you like to read and how does it affect the fiction you write?

A: I was an English major in college, but for pure love of science, I also took a wide range of science courses—everything from biochemistry to physics. To this day, I prefer to start my mornings by reading about the latest scientific research and discoveries. While I'll read just about anything under that umbrella, I'm particularly interested in immunology, anthropology, astronomy, and technological innovations in medicine. I suppose it comes as no surprise, then, that I tend to weave elements of science and technology into my fiction writing. What I enjoy most is using science as a jumping-off point to explore the human experience and the human psyche in a fictional context.

About the author

B.C. van Tol was grown in the Garden State. In her spare time—when she's not writing—she avidly consumes science fiction and fantasy in all forms. She also enjoys dabbling in watercolors and hiking with her husband and rescue dog.

bcvantol.com, @bcvantol

Copyright

Title information

Metaphorosis August 2020

ISSN: 2573-136X (online)
ISBN: 978-1-64076-175-9 (e-book)
ISBN: 978-1-64076-176-6 (paperback)

Copyright

Copyright ©2020, Metaphorosis Publishing.
Cover art © 2020 by Melissa Kojima.
http://www.melissakojima.net, @MelissaKojima

"Calling Me Home" © 2020, Spencer Nitkey
"Devilish Calliope and the Ungrooviest Apocalypse" ©
2020, Evan Marcroft
"All That Remains" © 2020, Michael Gardner
"Joy (Unplugged)" © 2020, B.C. van Tol

Authors also retain copyrights to all other material in the
anthology.

Works of fiction

This book contains works of fiction. Characters, dialogue, places, organizations, incidents, and events portrayed in the works are fictional and are products of the author's imagination or used fictitiously. Any resemblance to actual persons, places, organizations, or events is coincidental.

All rights reserved

All rights reserved. With the exception of brief quotations embedded in critical reviews, no part of this publication may be reproduced, distributed, stored, or transmitted in any form or by any means – including all electronic and mechanical means – without written permission from the publisher.

The authors and artists worked hard to create this work for your enjoyment. Please respect their work and their rights by using only authorized copies. If you would like to share this material with others, please buy them a copy.

Moral rights asserted

Each author whose work is included in this book has asserted their moral rights, including the right to be identified as the author of their respective work(s).

Publisher

Metaphorosis

a magazine of speculative fiction

Metaphorosis Magazine is an imprint of
Metaphorosis Publishing
Neskowin, OR, USA

www.metaphorosis.com

"Metaphorosis" is a registered trademark.

Discounts available

Substantial discounts are available for educational institutions, including writing workshops. Discounts are also available for quantity purchases. For details, contact Metaphorosis at metaphorosis.com/about

Metaphorosis Publishing

Metaphorosis offers beautifully written science fiction and fantasy. Our imprints include:

Metaphorosis Magazine
Plant Based Press
Verdage

You can also find us:
@MetaphorosisMag, @MetaphorosisRev,
@Metaphorosis
www.facebook.com/metaphorosis

Help keep Metaphorosis running by supporting us at
Patreon.com/metaphorosis

See more about some of our books on the following pages.

Metaphorosis

a magazine of speculative fiction

Metaphorosis is an online speculative fiction magazine dedicated to quality writing. We publish an original story every week, along with author bios, interviews, and notes on story origins.

We also publish monthly print and e-book issues, as well as yearly Best of and Complete anthologies.

Come and see us online at magazine.Metaphorosis.com

Metaphorosis:
Best of 2019

The best science fiction and fantasy stories from *Metaphorosis* magazine's fourth year.

Metaphorosis
2019

All the stories from *Metaphorosis* magazine's fourth year. Fifty-two great SFF stories.

Metaphorosis:
Best of 2018

The best science fiction and fantasy stories from *Metaphorosis* magazine's third year.

Metaphorosis
2018

All the stories from *Metaphorosis* magazine's third year. Fifty-two great SFF stories.

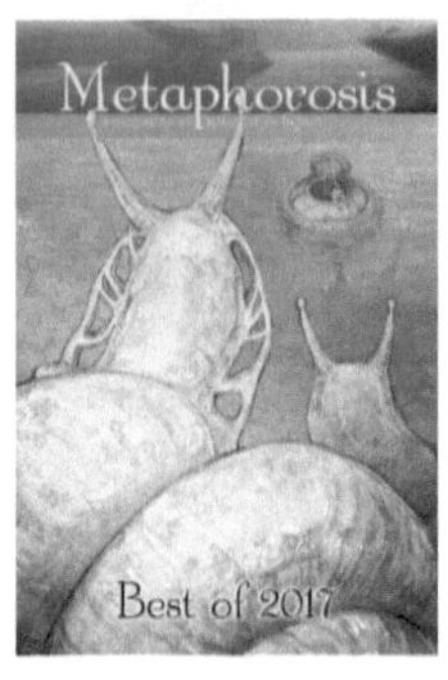

Metaphorosis:
Best of 2017

The best science fiction and fantasy stories from *Metaphorosis* magazine's *second* year.

Metaphorosis
2017

All the stories from *Metaphorosis* magazine's second year. Fifty-three great SFF stories.

Metaphorosis:
Best of 2016

The best science fiction and fantasy stories from *Metaphorosis* magazine's first year.

Metaphorosis
2016

Almost all the stories from *Metaphorosis* magazine's first year.

Plant Based Press

Vegan-friendly science fiction and fantasy, including an annual anthology of the year's best SFF stories.

Best Vegan SFF of 2019

The best vegan-friendly science fiction and fantasy stories of 2019!

Best Vegan SFF of 2018

The best vegan-friendly science fiction and fantasy stories of 2018!

Best Vegan SFF
of 2017

The best vegan-
friendly science
fiction and fantasy
stories of 2017!

Best Vegan SFF
of 2016

The best vegan-
friendly science
fiction and fantasy
stories of 2016!

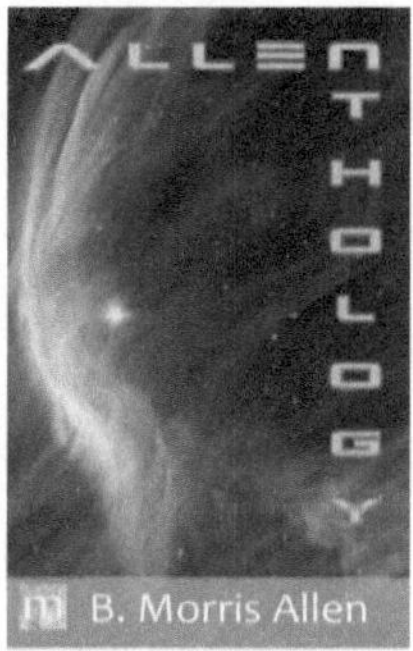

Susurrus

A darkly romantic story of magic, love, and suffering.

Allenthology: Volume I

A quarter century of SFF, including the full contents of the collections *Tocsin, Start with Stones,* and *Metaphorosis.*

Verdage

Science fiction and fantasy books for writers – full of great stories, often with an additional focus on the craft of speculative fiction writing.

Score

an SFF symphony

What if stories were written like music? *Score* is an anthology of varied stories arranged to follow an emotional score from the heights of joy to the depths of despair – but always with a little hope shining through.

Reading 5X5

Five stories, five times

Twenty-five SFF authors, five base stories, five versions of each – see how different writers take on the same material, with stories in contemporary and high fantasy, soft and hard SF, and a mysterious 'other' category.

Reading 5X5

Writers' Edition

All the stories from the regular, readers' edition, plus two extra stories, the story seed, and authors' notes on writing. Over 100 pages of additional material specifically aimed at writers.

www.ingramcontent.com/pod-product-compliance
Lightning Source LLC
Chambersburg PA
CBHW020332110726
47898CB00003B/838